108課綱、全民英檢初級適用

三版

基礎英文字彙力

2000 習題本

丁雍嫻 邢雯桂
盧思嘉 應惠蕙 編著

三民書局

目次

Level 1   Test 1—Test 40

嗨！你今天練習了嗎？

完成一回習題後，你可以在該回次的◯打勾並在 __80__ 填寫成績。

一起檢核英文實力吧！

Level 2　Test 1—Test 40

Level 1 Test 1

Class: _____ No.: _____ Name: _____ Score: _____

I. 文意字彙 (40%)

_____ 1. Kelly is a f_____t runner. She can run 100 meters in 10 seconds.

_____ 2. People must apply for the club card in p_____n. It can't be done over the phone.

_____ 3. Mr. Lin didn't know what to do when his car broke down in the m_____e of nowhere.

_____ 4. You can't fire Richard until you have found someone to take the p_____e of him.

_____ 5. After a month, Doris started to feel at h_____e with her new roommate.

II. 字彙配合 (請忽略大小寫) (40%)

(A) television	(B) become	(C) talk	(D) computer	(E) health

_____ 1. Are you available right now? We need to _____.

_____ 2. I don't know what will _____ of me if I don't pass the entrance exam.

_____ 3. We usually don't realize the importance of _____ until we lose it.

_____ 4. By using a _____, we can save at least half of the time on the paperwork.

_____ 5. May watched _____ instead of doing her homework all day long.

III. 選擇題 (20%)

_____ 1. This _____ is not sharp enough. Is it the only one we have?

    (A) health   (B) woman   (C) knife   (D) computer

_____ 2. We _____ Cindy as our leader because she was very responsible.

    (A) slowed   (B) chose   (C) talked   (D) topped

_____ 3. I'm surprised that Carol speaks Vietnamese so _____.

    (A) later   (B) there   (C) over   (D) well

_____ 4. Please _____ right at this corner. The hospital is over there.

    (A) turn   (B) become   (C) stab   (D) put

_____ 5. The school needed a _____ to teach students how to swim.

    (A) television   (B) church   (C) conversation   (D) trainer

Level 1 Test 2

Class: _____ No.: _____ Name: _____ Score: _____

I. 文意字彙 (40%)

_____ 1. Stanley t____ped over a rock on the sidewalk and fell down.

_____ 2. If the w____r is good tomorrow, we will go on a picnic in the park.

_____ 3. In the 18th century, only the middle c____s had enough money to buy their own houses.

_____ 4. For the f____t time in my life, I felt I was old enough to take care of myself.

_____ 5. The French fries were so delicious that I couldn't h____p but eat the entire bag.

II. 字彙配合 (請忽略大小寫) (40%)

(A) subject	(B) tree	(C) mind	(D) light	(E) tell

_____ 1. It is important to be able to _____ right from wrong.

_____ 2. You must _____ your language when you talk to the principal.

_____ 3. David's favorite _____ at school was history.

_____ 4. Dad used a match to _____ the candles on the cake.

_____ 5. Louisa used to read under this _____ when she was a child.

III. 選擇題 (20%)

_____ 1. When my best friend left for the United States, I went to the airport to _____ her off.

    (A) see   (B) mind   (C) bug   (D) tell

_____ 2. Becky was _____ with me for not keeping her secret.

    (A) dark   (B) clear   (C) heavy   (D) angry

_____ 3. Mr. Lopez decided to buy the _____ because it was near the train station.

    (A) ocean   (B) tree   (C) house   (D) baby

_____ 4. Jeff is always kind to me, so I can't turn my _____ on him when he needs me.

    (A) subject   (B) front   (C) back   (D) lot

_____ 5. Nelson made _____ of his free time to learn German and Spanish.

    (A) right   (B) use   (C) job   (D) sea

Level 1 Test 3

Class: _____ No.: _____ Name: _____ Score: _____

I. 文意字彙 (40%)

_____ 1. The secretary was asked to t____e the letter within one hour.

_____ 2. The milk went bad and gave off a sour s____l.

_____ 3. My husband and I are b____h interested in classical music.

_____ 4. We went on a trip to the mountains to enjoy the beauty of n____e.

_____ 5. It a____rs that Matthew and Lora are in love with each other.

II. 字彙配合 (請忽略大小寫) (40%)

(A) team	(B) cost	(C) wore	(D) ate	(E) will

_____ 1. The bridge was built at a(n) _____ of about three billion dollars.

_____ 2. Anthony finally finished the difficult task with his strong _____.

_____ 3. The great medical expenses _____ up most of Andrew's money.

_____ 4. Sandra _____ a white shirt and a black skirt to work today.

_____ 5. A football _____ usually consists of eleven players.

III. 選擇題 (20%)

_____ 1. Jimmy _____ an electric guitar as his Christmas gift.

(A) ate　　(B) wanted　　(C) drove　　(D) wore

_____ 2. It took me about 5 minutes to walk from here _____ the supermarket.

(A) to　　(B) above　　(C) below　　(D) along

_____ 3. This evening gown is too _____ for Susan. It's not her size.

(A) warm　　(B) north　　(C) only　　(D) small

_____ 4. Our city needs more green spaces like _____, not shopping centers.

(A) teams　　(B) wills　　(C) parks　　(D) calls

_____ 5. For one _____, Susan didn't invite me. For another, I didn't want to go, anyway.

(A) thing　　(B) cost　　(C) now　　(D) drive

Level 1 Test 4

Class: _____ No.: _____ Name: _____ Score: _____

I. 文意字彙 (40%)

_____ 1. The clothing store is in the c_____r of the town, so it's convenient to get there.

_____ 2. I have been cooking dinner for a whole week. Let's eat at a Thai restaurant for a c_____e tonight.

_____ 3. Debbie noted down my phone number on a piece of p_____r.

_____ 4. H_____r hard the task is, I will try my best to complete it.

_____ 5. The student always s_____ies hard to get good grades.

II. 字彙配合 (請忽略大小寫) (40%)

(A) deal	(B) week	(C) buy	(D) clean	(E) way

_____ 1. The Wang family have to _____ out their house since they are moving next Monday.

_____ 2. I am not going to _____ the car. It is too expensive.

_____ 3. Watching Korean dramas is a good _____ to learn Korean.

_____ 4. There are seven days in a _____.

_____ 5. Sandra can _____ with her stress well.

III. 選擇題 (20%)

_____ 1. The fishermen are _____ for tuna in the ocean.

    (A) selling   (B) drying   (C) inhabiting   (D) fishing

_____ 2. The _____ old man did not have enough money to pay for his lunch.

    (A) wide   (B) deep   (C) poor   (D) hard

_____ 3. Thousands of _____ came to attend the rock music festival.

    (A) ways   (B) people   (C) weeks   (D) deals

_____ 4. Stephen King is a well-known _____ of novels.

    (A) writer   (B) buy   (C) clean   (D) world

_____ 5. Getting enough sleep is _____ for your health.

    (A) shallow   (B) good   (C) soft   (D) beautiful

Level 1 Test 5

Class: _____ No.: _____ Name: _____ Score: _____

I. 文意字彙 (40%)

_____ 1. An a_____t is a place where you can find many airplanes.

_____ 2. Steve finally s_____wed up when the party was nearly over.

_____ 3. Jim didn't clearly e_____n the reason why he was late.

_____ 4. I believe you have the a_____y to finish the work by yourself.

_____ 5. The fighting must be brought to an end as s_____n as possible.

II. 字彙配合 (請忽略大小寫) (40%)

(A) road	(B) art	(C) child	(D) excellent	(E) real

_____ 1. Teresa developed _____ drawing skills at a young age.

_____ 2. Sophie hated vegetables when she was a(n) _____.

_____ 3. Jenny helped an old man cross the _____.

_____ 4. Dancing and singing are two kinds of _____ forms.

_____ 5. Snoopy is a cartoon character. He doesn't exist in the _____ world.

III. 選擇題 (20%)

_____ 1. Jason can _____ delicious apple pies.

　　(A) build　　　　(B) open　　　　(C) require　　　　(D) make

_____ 2. The dogs were completely _____ of control when they smelled their favorite food.

　　(A) in　　　　(B) out　　　　(C) very　　　　(D) close

_____ 3. France and Portugal are the _____ that border Spain.

　　(A) whites　　　　(B) doctors　　　　(C) countries　　　　(D) children

_____ 4. After the storm, the house was in poor condition, so it was in _____ of repair.

　　(A) need　　　　(B) road　　　　(C) heart　　　　(D) blue

_____ 5. Please close the _____ when you leave.

　　(A) door　　　　(B) doc　　　　(C) kid　　　　(D) tea

Level 1 Test 6

Class: _____ No.: _____ Name: _____ Score: _____

I. 文意字彙 (40%)

_____ 1. The king has the right to e____e power over his subjects.

_____ 2. The engineer promised that he would solve the problem right a____y.

_____ 3. When Bill finally arrived, we had a____y finished the work.

_____ 4. The number of the s____ts in my class is 45.

_____ 5. I think the poem can be explained in a completely d____t way.

II. 字彙配合 (請忽略大小寫) (40%)

(A) bread	(B) gives	(C) follows	(D) dreams	(E) history

_____ 1. Emily often _____ in to her sweet tooth and eats lots of chocolate.

_____ 2. Tim sometimes _____ about being chased by a dog.

_____ 3. The saying "_____ repeats itself" means things often happen in the same way as they did before.

_____ 4. You can buy freshly baked _____ at this bakery every afternoon.

_____ 5. The prize winners are as _____—John, Mary, and Lily.

III. 選擇題 (20%)

_____ 1. Robin likes quiet places and goes fishing at the lake _____ now and then.

(A) every   (B) mean   (C) more   (D) similar

_____ 2. We must not talk on the phone while driving. We should always pay attention to the possible dangers in any _____.

(A) history   (B) case   (C) bread   (D) red

_____ 3. The phrase "paint the town red" _____ "go out and have fun with friends."

(A)follows   (B) attacks   (C) gives   (D) means

_____ 4. The paintings on display are _____ together by size.

(A) hidden   (B) salted   (C) grouped   (D) dreamed

_____ 5. The CEO said that there would be a pay _____ of 10% for employees who failed to reach the goal.

(A) dream   (B) cut   (C) attack   (D) mother

Level 1 Test 7

Class: _____ No.: _____ Name: _____ Score: _____

I. 文意字彙 (40%)

_____ 1. It is i_____t that you should think carefully before making the final decision.

_____ 2. This terrorist attack scared Tom for l_____e.

_____ 3. The police searched the dark woods in the h_____e of finding the movie star's missing son.

_____ 4. Jerry sat n_____t to a pretty lady on the bus this morning.

_____ 5. Susan is such a f_____y person that all of her classmates like her.

II. 字彙配合 (請忽略大小寫) (40%)

(A) broke	(B) kept	(C) family	(D) dropped	(E) death

_____ 1. It was too bad that our car _____ down on a mountain road.

_____ 2. Although Mrs. Miller felt very tired after work, she still cooked dinner for her _____.

_____ 3. You may be put to _____ for selling drugs in certain countries.

_____ 4. My grandfather was forced to _____ out of school when World War II broke out.

_____ 5. Sickness _____ Sally from going to the Christmas party.

III. 選擇題 (20%)

_____ 1. Ms. Brown _____ her own restaurant at the age of 25.

(A) upped (B) started (C) checked (D) schooled

_____ 2. It's difficult for Daniel to make a _____ between the two jobs.

(A) family (B) bill (C) must (D) choice

_____ 3. Do you _____ when Aunt Susan moved to Seattle?

(A) know (B) break (C) begin (D) keep

_____ 4. Which _____ would you prefer, bananas or papayas?

(A) bank (B) fruit (C) day (D) drop

_____ 5. The weather was very good, so we made some sandwiches and had a picnic in the _____.

(A) death (B) night (C) sun (D) eye

Level 1 Test 8

Class: _____ No.: _____ Name: _____ Score: _____

I. 文意字彙 (40%)

_____ 1. I carry an umbrella with me j_____t in case it may rain.

_____ 2. Joseph is good at growing fruit. He is a b_____n gardener.

_____ 3. Lora always seems so happy and f_____l of life.

_____ 4. Teresa's selfless love for all the people around her sets a good
e_____e for us.

_____ 5. The post office and the bank are built on the m_____n street of
the small town.

II. 字彙配合 (請忽略大小寫) (40%)

(A) courses	(B) where	(C) cookies	(D) when	(E) animals

_____ 1. You can find many different kinds of _____ in the zoo.

_____ 2. I found a café _____ we can meet for coffee.

_____ 3. The handmade _____ of the bakery are my favorite.

_____ 4. Mary took many _____ at college and learned much about science.

_____ 5. I'll call you _____ I reach the airport.

III. 選擇題 (20%)

_____ 1. The new department store is due to _____ this weekend.

    (A) look   (B) act   (C) open   (D) leave

_____ 2. Laura looked slim in the _____ dress.

    (A) black   (B) closed   (C) interested   (D) warm

_____ 3. Jeff spent a lot of _____ on video games.

    (A) cold   (B) money   (C) east   (D) fat

_____ 4. Wendy reads _____ to her son every night.

    (A) cookies   (B) animals   (C) stories   (D) men

_____ 5. Housing has become a very _____ problem in this country.

    (A) shut   (B) serious   (C) thin   (D) bored

Level 1 Test 9

Class: _____ No.: _____ Name: _____ Score: _____

I. 文意字彙 (40%)

_____ 1. Judy likes to listen to some soft m____c while she is doing her homework.

_____ 2. I prefer to go to a l____e show rather than watch videos online.

_____ 3. M____n technology has greatly improved the standard of living.

_____ 4. All the m____rs of this club have the right to use the swimming pool.

_____ 5. Paula loves to pour cold w____r on everybody's plans or ideas.

II. 字彙配合 (請忽略大小寫) (40%)

(A) either	(B) about	(C) across	(D) far	(E) ago

_____ 1. It is just a small river. Perhaps we can swim _____.

_____ 2. The band's new album is _____ better than their last one.

_____ 3. Ronald went to study in the United States ten years _____.

_____ 4. Ivan doesn't like fast food and his sister doesn't, _____.

_____ 5. Peggy waited for her boyfriend for _____ twenty minutes.

III. 選擇題 (20%)

_____ 1. The math problem was so _____ that Sarah solved it right away.

(A) either   (B) each   (C) easy   (D) up-to-date

_____ 2. The teacher wanted to _____ out why Jerry was afraid of speaking English.

(A) play   (B) find   (C) hold   (D) kill

_____ 3. There is some paint on the artist's _____.

(A) face   (B) camera   (C) grass   (D) news

_____ 4. Mr. Chen is _____ to speak five foreign languages.

(A) hard   (B) far   (C) difficult   (D) able

_____ 5. In this village, the _____ are taught to respect and learn from old people.

(A) newscast   (B) killer   (C) head   (D) young

Level 1 Test 10

Class: _____ No.: _____ Name: _____ Score: _____

I. 文意字彙 (40%)

_____ 1. Henry b_____ed that he had already known what had happened. In fact, he knew nothing about it.

_____ 2. Zack failed to hand in his homework on t_____e.

_____ 3. Melanie got e_____n with Fred by dating another guy after he had cheated on her.

_____ 4. This is my personal business. I don't want to talk about it in p_____c.

_____ 5. Nick was a little hungry, so he ate a c_____e bar.

II. 字彙配合 (請忽略大小寫) (40%)

(A) as	(B) without	(C) machine	(D) but	(E) body

_____ 1. Although you cannot speak English, you can use _____ language to express yourself.

_____ 2. Mr. Perez bought a washing _____ so that he didn't have to wash clothes by hand.

_____ 3. Tiffany used her hat _____ a basket when she gathered berries in the forest.

_____ 4. It was rude of Tom to use my pen _____ asking.

_____ 5. Nobody _____ Riley noticed my new glasses.

III. 選擇題 (20%)

_____ 1. Matthew _____ his wife singing happily in the bathroom.

    (A) heard   (B) reasoned   (C) moved   (D) landed

_____ 2. Mr. Walker's condition went from _____ to worse after he moved to New York.

    (A) expensive   (B) bad   (C) private   (D) several

_____ 3. Cuba is a(n) _____ country.

    (A) body   (B) movement   (C) sequence   (D) island

_____ 4. We don't like John because he _____ telling dirty jokes.

    (A) orders   (B) numbers   (C) enjoys   (D) drops

_____ 5. This restaurant is famous for its cheap and delicious _____.

    (A) earth   (B) food   (C) front   (D) machine

Level 1 Test 11

Class: _____ No.: _____ Name: _____ Score: _____

I. 文意字彙 (40%)

_____ 1. Ian has stopped smoking e_____r since his first child was born.

_____ 2. Peter seemed to f_____t a losing battle against cancer.

_____ 3. If a house needs to be cleaned h_____e and there, it needs to be cleaned in several different places.

_____ 4. I have no i_____a how these country folks celebrate the birth of a baby.

_____ 5. We must learn to make the m_____t of the time we have.

II. 字彙配合 (請忽略大小寫) (40%)

(A) problem	(B) newspaper	(C) green	(D) high	(E) meat

_____ 1. Mr. Jackson has a habit of reading the _____ while he is having breakfast.

_____ 2. It is good for elderly people to eat more vegetables and less _____.

_____ 3. The engineer found a small _____ in the system and fixed it right away.

_____ 4. I was _____ with envy when Mary showed me her new phone.

_____ 5. Michael got a very _____ grade on his math exam.

III. 選擇題 (20%)

_____ 1. It was _____ cold that I couldn't feel anything in my hands.

    (A) yet   (B) so   (C) too   (D) least

_____ 2. If you don't hurry up, you'll be _____ for school again.

    (A) old   (B) high   (C) low   (D) late

_____ 3. Henry always makes detailed _____ before he takes a trip.

    (A) newspapers   (B) cars   (C) plans   (D) problems

_____ 4. Andy _____ some tomatoes in his little garden.

    (A) worked   (B) bridged   (C) tested   (D) grew

_____ 5. The government is going to build a new highway in the near _____.

    (A) future   (B) fun   (C) green   (D) meat

Level 1 Test 12

Class: _____ No.: _____ Name: _____ Score: _____

I. 文意字彙 (40%)

_____ 1. Owen is easy-going. His brother, on the other h_____d, is not very friendly.

_____ 2. People visit this famous temple all y_____r round.

_____ 3. Linda worked hard all day and finished her homework at l_____t.

_____ 4. The boy was h_____f dead from walking for a very long time.

_____ 5. This song is especially p_____r with the working class.

II. 字彙配合 (請忽略大小寫) (40%)

(A) filed	(B) area	(C) fell	(D) picture	(E) media

_____ 1. John and Julie's marriage _____ apart because of their different views on money.

_____ 2. The movie star's wedding received a lot of _____ attention.

_____ 3. I took a(n) _____ of the beautiful rainbow and posted it online.

_____ 4. Eric had _____ away his notes and photographs.

_____ 5. The sign indicates that hunting is not allowed in this _____.

III. 選擇題 (20%)

_____ 1. My sister doesn't _____ me use her computer.

    (A) file   (B) do   (C) picture   (D) let

_____ 2. Richard has always had a great _____ in cooking.

    (A) interest   (B) city   (C) area   (D) rise

_____ 3. The building project was stopped, most _____ because of safety concerns.

    (A) never   (B) probably   (C) first   (D) much

_____ 4. Ted was _____ about what would be the most effective way to get stronger.

    (A) falling   (B) thinking   (C) grounding   (D) aging

_____ 5. Nora was sitting on her brother's _____, teaching him how to play the piano.

    (A) media   (B) glass   (C) left   (D) ground

Level 1 Test 13

Class: _____ No.: _____ Name: _____ Score: _____

I. 文意字彙 (40%)

_____ 1. Please wait here and don't leave. I will be back in a s_____d.

_____ 2. Don't worry about Edward; he is old e_____h to take care of himself.

_____ 3. Bill burst out laughing when he saw Fanny having her sweater on i_____d out.

_____ 4. If you give up your job now, how are you going to make a living for the r_____t of your life?

_____ 5. Although the two kids look a_____t the same, their parents can still tell who is who.

II. 字彙配合 (請忽略大小寫) (40%)

(A) player	(B) booked	(C) movie	(D) took	(E) drank

_____ 1. We can't have dinner in the Japanese restaurant because it is _____ up every evening this month.

_____ 2. Patrick felt thirsty and _____ a can of beer.

_____ 3. The new _____ soon became a hit, and many people wanted to see it.

_____ 4. Henry is considered to be the best _____ on the basketball team.

_____ 5. Feeling hot, Sue _____ off her coat and put it on the sofa.

III. 選擇題 (20%)

_____ 1. My cousin is a soldier, and he has many _____ stories to tell about his life in the army.

    (A) interesting   (B) sad   (C) boring   (D) long

_____ 2. Henry _____ Dolores so much that he is willing to do anything for her.

    (A) books   (B) loves   (C) learns   (D) takes

_____ 3. Susan was _____ to meet her old friends again.

    (A) healthy   (B) special   (C) short   (D) happy

_____ 4. The names of authors are _____ on page 275.

    (A) colored   (B) drunk   (C) listed   (D) hated

_____ 5. Ares is the ancient Greek _____ of war.

    (A) film   (B) god   (C) player   (D) library

Level 1 Test 14

Class: _____ No.: _____ Name: _____ Score: _____

I. 文意字彙 (40%)

_____ 1. The parents finally stopped worrying when their son got home
s____e and sound.

_____ 2. This article clearly explains why oil prices are on the r____e
again.

_____ 3. Charlie studied from m____g till night in the hope of passing the
history exam.

_____ 4. Jeremy played basketball very well and was chosen to be a
member of the n____l team.

_____ 5. We may not be able to finish the work on time; as a m____r of
fact, we are two weeks behind schedule.

II. 字彙配合 (請忽略大小寫) (40%)

(A) coffee	(B) practiced	(C) passed	(D) language	(E) market

_____ 1. The doctor has _____ medicine for twenty years ever since he completed his
training.

_____ 2. Lydia always buys a cup of _____ on her way to work.

_____ 3. The police officer could tell from the man's body _____ that he was lying.

_____ 4. John bought a new alarm clock at the _____.

_____ 5. The girl nearly _____ out when she saw a dead body in the river.

III. 選擇題 (20%)

_____ 1. You can click the _____ arrow to move to the bottom of the page.

(A) many (B) large (C) down (D) unkind

_____ 2. The box is so _____ that I cannot move it on my own.

(A) light (B) kind (C) heavy (D) small

_____ 3. Eunice keeps three _____, including a dog, a cat, and a bird.

(A) pets (B) mountains (C) languages (D) fathers

_____ 4. After a long talk with him, I _____ that Kevin was an honest person.

(A) fell (B) felt (C) started (D) practiced

_____ 5. The manager had a heart attack at the _____ of the meeting.

(A) coffee (B) million (C) market (D) end

Level 1 Test 15

Class: _____ No.: _____ Name: _____ Score: _____

I. 文意字彙 (40%)

_____ 1. It's difficult to brush your teeth and speak at o____e.

_____ 2. Linda put on her white dress, getting r____y for the party in the evening.

_____ 3. Ms. Lin asked her students to write an article no l____s than 300 words.

_____ 4. William came up with a f____h idea and helped us solve the problem in a different way.

_____ 5. I always buy fruit and vegetables that are in s____n because they are cheap and delicious.

II. 字彙配合 (請忽略大小寫) (40%)

(A) point	(B) line	(C) get	(D) rock	(E) level

_____ 1. After the earthquake, the road was blocked by a huge _____.

_____ 2. This book was written especially for learners at the basic _____.

_____ 3. How can you _____ along with such a selfish person?

_____ 4. The president needs someone who can _____ out his mistakes.

_____ 5. The students were asked to _____ up while waiting for the school bus.

III. 選擇題 (20%)

_____ 1. The new king came to _____ after his father passed away.

    (A) knowledge   (B) power   (C) rock   (D) oil

_____ 2. The _____ man lifted the heavy box easily.

    (A) low   (B) more   (C) high   (D) strong

_____ 3. There are 24 hours in a _____.

    (A) point   (B) line   (C) day   (D) dog

_____ 4. Bill has always wanted to visit the British _____ in London.

    (A) Museum   (B) Level   (C) Mouth   (D) Night

_____ 5. This cancer drug can _____ many people from death.

    (A) shock   (B) save   (C) prepare   (D) say

Level 1 Test 16

Class: _____ No.: _____ Name: _____ Score: _____

I. 文意字彙 (40%)

_____ 1. Pamela put some pot p_____ts on the balcony of her new apartment.

_____ 2. My neighbor gave me some s_____ds, saying that they would grow into beautiful flowers.

_____ 3. This robot has too many parts. I don't know how to put them t_____r.

_____ 4. The final r_____t is due by next Friday; anyone who does not hand it in on time will fail the course.

_____ 5. The small island is f_____s for its special wild animals.

II. 字彙配合 (請忽略大小寫) (40%)

(A) since	(B) parted	(C) by	(D) put	(E) picked

_____ 1. Tina and her family traveled across America _____ car last month.

_____ 2. We managed to _____ out the fire before it burned down the house.

_____ 3. I haven't seen Betty _____ last Christmas.

_____ 4. Irena decided to quit her job because her boss _____ on her all the time.

_____ 5. Willy has already _____ with his old bike and bought a new one.

III. 選擇題 (20%)

_____ 1. I enjoy watching the evening news _____ to learn about current events.

 (A) program   (B) hairstyle   (C) role   (D) name

_____ 2. Jessica _____ long hours preparing for the job interview.

 (A) bought   (B) placed   (C) spent   (D) brought

_____ 3. This _____ street is only a few meters long.

 (A) online   (B) short   (C) still   (D) rich

_____ 4. Mrs. Chen has a new _____, and it makes her look younger.

 (A) hairdo   (B) part   (C) nothing   (D) third

_____ 5. Laura _____ her old guitar to her friend for 1,000 NT dollars.

 (A) put   (B) named   (C) picked   (D) sold

Level 1 Test 17

Class: _____ No.: _____ Name: _____ Score: _____

I. 文意字彙 (40%)

_____ 1. In the p____t, women couldn't receive education.

_____ 2. These animals usually s____e food for the winter in a safe place.

_____ 3. The teacher r____ed her eyes from the book and looked at the student who was using a smartphone.

_____ 4. I think both the food and s____e in the French restaurant are great.

_____ 5. Mr. Lin stopped to make c____n that every student understood what he had said.

II. 字彙配合 (請忽略大小寫) (40%)

(A) under	(B) whether	(C) off	(D) before	(E) though

_____ 1. Different animals have lived on this island long _____ humans came.

_____ 2. _____ we can go on a picnic or not depends on the weather.

_____ 3. Mr. Parker wiped _____ the tears from his partner's face.

_____ 4. _____ the soldiers are young, they are very brave in battle.

_____ 5. The show is for adults only. People _____ eighteen are not allow to watch.

III. 選擇題 (20%)

_____ 1. This musician wrote many pop _____ for several famous singers.

(A) offices   (B) sides   (C) rivers   (D) songs

_____ 2. It took climbers 6 hours to _____ the mountain top.

(A) have   (B) pay   (C) reach   (D) ship

_____ 3. Ted speaks French. He _____ speaks Japanese.

(A) least   (B) really   (C) though   (D) also

_____ 4. This jacket is too _____ for Emma to wear. She needs a smaller one.

(A) big   (B) off   (C) sure   (D) least

_____ 5. You can make the _____ in cash or by credit card.

(A) no   (B) someone   (C) payment   (D) side

Level 1 Test 18

Class: _____ No.: _____ Name: _____ Score: _____

I. 文意字彙 (40%)

_____ 1. It was very crowded in the museum, so Jessie went o____e to get some fresh air.

_____ 2. The killer is serving a life s____e in prison.

_____ 3. Is it p____e that you may have left your wallet at home instead of losing it?

_____ 4. I suggest that we have dinner at the newly-opened Japanese r____t.

_____ 5. Because of s____e, we know the connection between rain and rainbow.

II. 字彙配合 (請忽略大小寫) (40%)

(A) thin	(B) if	(C) or	(D) new	(E) although

_____ 1. _____ there were no flowers and trees, the world would look dull and ugly.

_____ 2. Charlie became very _____ after he recovered from the serious disease.

_____ 3. _____ it is very cold, all members in the track and field team show up for practice on time.

_____ 4. Kevin likes this old blanket a lot. He doesn't want to buy a _____ one.

_____ 5. It takes five hours _____ so to go from Taipei to Kaohsiung by train.

III. 選擇題 (20%)

_____ 1. Eric is good at math, therefore this question is a(n) _____ of cake for him.
(A) piece (B) egg (C) newlywed (D) sound

_____ 2. The ticket price is high, but it doesn't _____ Ella from going to the musical.
(A) wind (B) come (C) stop (D) share

_____ 3. _____ the summer vacation, many students have to work for their school fee.
(A) Round (B) During (C) Inside (D) Around

_____ 4. Helen just left the party without a(n) _____.
(A) size (B) air (C) today (D) word

_____ 5. This book is about how to run a _____.
(A) noise (B) share (C) set (D) business

Level 1 Test 19

Class: _____ No.: _____ Name: _____ Score: _____

I. 文意字彙 (40%)

_____ 1. These students haven't fully u_____d what this sentence means.

_____ 2. It is d_____t to tell the differences between the two pictures. They look exactly the same.

_____ 3. I am pretty s_____e that I brought my wallet with me when I left home.

_____ 4. W_____h kind of ice cream do you prefer, chocolate or mango?

_____ 5. Please leave enough s_____e for this sofa. It is really large.

II. 字彙配合 (請忽略大小寫) (40%)

(A) free	(B) while	(C) shape	(D) sign	(E) sometimes

_____ 1. There is a _____ saying that the airport is closed because of the typhoon.

_____ 2. Lily was mad at Kevin for keeping her waiting for a long _____.

_____ 3. If you buy four cans of beer, you can get one for _____.

_____ 4. Jane made chocolate in the _____ of heart as a Valentine's Day gift for her boyfriend.

_____ 5. Anna doesn't drink tea. She drinks coffee _____.

III. 選擇題 (20%)

_____ 1. Not _____ likes this movie. Some people love it, but some hate it.

(A) another (B) same (C) hers (D) everyone

_____ 2. There are many old buildings in this ancient _____.

(A) indication (B) care (C) town (D) common

_____ 3. The little _____ who is wearing a brown jacket is my younger brother.

(A) teacher (B) boy (C) like (D) try

_____ 4. This test is pretty _____. Tim finished it in 5 minutes.

(A) common (B) certain (C) south (D) simple

_____ 5. Mr. Smith asked his students to go to his office one after _____.

(A) rare (B) another (C) easy (D) free

Level 1 Test 20

Class: _____ No.: _____ Name: _____ Score: _____

I. 文意字彙 (40%)

_____ 1. Smoking is not a _____ wed in public places.

_____ 2. Miranda became a world-famous singer in her e_____y twenties.

_____ 3. For your safety, you have to follow the t_____c rules.

_____ 4. My friends usually pay me a v_____t on Friday nights.

_____ 5. Christian likes pudding because of its sweet t_____e.

II. 字彙配合 (請忽略大小寫) (40%)

(A) own	(B) west	(C) again	(D) other	(E) few

_____ 1. Susan didn't understand what I said, so I explained to her once _____.

_____ 2. The Franks moved to a bigger house, so their two kids can have their _____ rooms.

_____ 3. The poor man has nothing _____ than the old bicycle.

_____ 4. There are quite a _____ differences between American English and British English.

_____ 5. The post office is 400 meters _____ of the bank.

III. 選擇題 (20%)

_____ 1. Sam _____ goes to the art museum when he needs ideas for writing.

    (A) often   (B) am   (C) then   (D) late

_____ 2. Today is a _____ day, so the park is full of people.

    (A) west   (B) sunny   (C) best   (D) many

_____ 3. Great _____ in summer is dangerous for people who work outside.

    (A) game   (B) heat   (C) flavor   (D) ice

_____ 4. Ms. Brown asked her students to use _____ to support their ideas.

    (A) facts   (B) cans   (C) goes   (D) races

_____ 5. Without enough money, the team couldn't _____ out this project.

    (A) permit   (B) carry   (C) sing   (D) own

Level 1 Test 21

Class: _____ No.: _____ Name: _____ Score: _____

I. 文意字彙 (40%)

_____ 1. All the employees must attend the m_____g on time.

_____ 2. People who are near-sighted need to wear g_____s to help them see more clearly.

_____ 3. Please speak louder. I cannot hear your v_____e with so much noise around.

_____ 4. The student who fell of the stairs was brought to the h_____l.

_____ 5. After Ashley finished her h_____k, she helped her parents prepare for the dinner.

II. 字彙配合 (請忽略大小寫) (40%)

(A) waved	(B) asked	(C) question	(D) piano	(E) sent

_____ 1. The medical bill was too expensive. Without _____, this poor man couldn't paid for it.

_____ 2. When Lisa saw me, she _____ at me excitedly.

_____ 3. Tyler was _____ to buy lunch for the manager.

_____ 4. Gina can play several instruments, and _____ is one of them.

_____ 5. The tourist got lost and _____ the police about the way to his hotel.

III. 選擇題 (20%)

_____ 1. You have to sleep on the _____, for I don't have an extra bed.

    (A) answer   (B) tooth   (C) sofa   (D) goodbye

_____ 2. During the holiday season, _____ of people poured into the airport.

    (A) feet   (B) thousands   (C) cents   (D) drums

_____ 3. The shoe store held a _____ to clear out last season's products.

    (A) couch   (B) answer   (C) sale   (D) worry

_____ 4. Michael is careful of his behavior. He knows his kids _____ what he does.

    (A) copy   (B) drum   (C) foot   (D) trouble

_____ 5. My son is _____ at me for missing his baseball game.

    (A) medium   (B) all right   (C) O.K.   (D) mad

Level 1 Test 22

Class: _____ No.: _____ Name: _____ Score: _____

I. 文意字彙 (40%)

_____ 1. Ed and Anne went to s_____e quiet so they could talk.

_____ 2. Our classes usually begin at eight o_____k every morning.

_____ 3. In this hospital, v_____rs are not welcomed after 10:00 p.m.

_____ 4. The g_____r spoiled his granddaughter by letting her get her way.

_____ 5. Peter went to school without eating b_____t this morning.

II. 字彙配合 (請忽略大小寫) (40%)

(A) moon	(B) minute	(C) corner	(D) wrote	(E) watched

_____ 1. Christmas is around the _____. It is time to go shopping.

_____ 2. Buck's friend _____ over his baggage while he was buying the train tickets.

_____ 3. The player made a miraculous goal at the last _____ to win the game.

_____ 4. Mr. Huang _____ down the date of the test on the blackboard.

_____ 5. You will never lose weight if you only exercise once in a blue _____.

III. 選擇題 (20%)

_____ 1. The weather is so nice that I feel like going on a _____ in the park.

    (A) picnic   (B) reader   (C) hobby   (D) lake

_____ 2. The new medicine worked like _____, and the patient recovered in a very short time.

    (A) dull   (B) weak   (C) bright   (D) magic

_____ 3. Elle loves _____, but her brother hates it because of the smell.

    (A) honey   (B) sugar   (C) cheese   (D) weakness

_____ 4. This Chinese restaurant is famous for its roast _____.

    (A) duck   (B) seat   (C) lake   (D) reader

_____ 5. Greg's school is 2 _____ from his home, so he leaves early for school.

    (A) lakes   (B) hours   (C) seats   (D) hobbies

Level 1 Test 23

Class: _____ No.: _____ Name: _____ Score: _____

I. 文意字彙 (40%)

_____ 1. The lady p_____y asked the waiter to give her a glass of water.

_____ 2. It looks like rain. I g_____s that the baseball game will be called off.

_____ 3. This system is r_____y new compared with other systems. I don't know how to use it.

_____ 4. The child's death made the father w_____e up to his foolishness.

_____ 5. Leon got too nervous to answer any question in his first job i_____w.

II. 字彙配合 (請忽略大小寫) (40%)

(A) key	(B) parents	(C) chance	(D) fingers	(E) officer

_____ 1. The police _____ got hurt when she was on duty.

_____ 2. The _____ proudly watched their child perform on stage.

_____ 3. Whenever Brenda gets the _____, she goes on camping with friends.

_____ 4. There is no doubt that hard work is the _____ to success.

_____ 5. I am going to take part in the speech contest. Would you cross your _____ for me?

III. 選擇題 (20%)

_____ 1. After Tim heard the joke, he _____ out loud.

    (A) stood   (B) bore   (C) held   (D) laughed

_____ 2. Leslie couldn't sleep last night, so she tried to count _____.

    (A) milk   (B) yellow   (C) sheep   (D) homemaker

_____ 3. The children visited the _____ last Saturday. They were excited to see many animals.

    (A) neck   (B) bus   (C) housewife   (D) zoo

_____ 4. Emma read her report carefully to look for spelling _____.

    (A) errors   (B) necks   (C) buses   (D) yards

_____ 5. The spread of the disease is a hot _____ in recent news.

    (A) clerk   (B) topic   (C) parent   (D) yellow

Level 1 Test 24

Class: _____ No.: _____ Name: _____ Score: _____

I. 文意字彙 (40%)

_____ 1. The boy has made up his mind to study Western m_____e in the future.

_____ 2. I am s_____y that you lost your job.

_____ 3. As the French enjoy their wine, the English enjoy their a_____n tea.

_____ 4. This a_____e is scheduled to take off in three hours.

_____ 5. The cheesecake looks i_____g. May I have one small piece?

II. 字彙配合 (請忽略大小寫) (40%)

(A) add	(B) zero	(C) begin	(D) touch	(E) action

_____ 1. I can't possibly go to the United States. To _____ with, I have no time, and besides, I have no money.

_____ 2. The damage of the typhoon is predicted to _____ up to NT$20,000,000.

_____ 3. If people don't take _____ to protect these animals, they may die out soon.

_____ 4. Nelson tried to keep in _____ with his old friends on social media.

_____ 5. It is twenty degrees below _____ now. It is freezing cold.

III. 選擇題 (20%)

_____ 1. The weather was very good yesterday. There was no _____ in the sky.

(A) mouse   (B) cloud   (C) leg   (D) net

_____ 2. The man looks familiar to me, but I cannot _____ his name.

(A) pen   (B) row   (C) please   (D) remember

_____ 3. _____ and love are opposite in meaning.

(A) Cup   (B) Beginning   (C) Evening   (D) Hate

_____ 4. At the wedding, the bride _____ with her father. It made many people cry.

(A) rowed   (B) capped   (C) danced   (D) loved

_____ 5. It was too cold. Tina wore a pair of pants instead of a _____ to work.

(A) skirt   (B) plane   (C) beginning   (D) nought

Level 1 Test 25

Class: _____ No.: _____ Name: _____ Score: _____

I. 文意字彙 (40%)

_____ 1. Students must follow school r_____es, or they will be punished.

_____ 2. People are not allowed to s_____e here. If you need to do it, please go outside.

_____ 3. When Jim started to work, he moved into the a_____t near his office.

_____ 4. The children of my uncle and aunt are my c_____ns.

_____ 5. It was an e_____g game. Both players were talented and strong.

II. 字彙配合 (請忽略大小寫) (40%)

(A) round	(B) whose	(C) anything	(D) nobody	(E) below

_____ 1. Please write down your opinion about your shopping experience _____ this line.

_____ 2. If you touch me, try to hurt me or _____, I'll scream.

_____ 3. Ben has a dream of sailing _____ the world.

_____ 4. They are Mr. and Mrs. Brown, _____ car was stolen last week.

_____ 5. I felt like a _____ when I was sitting among all those famous and rich people.

III. 選擇題 (20%)

_____ 1. The policeman _____ with a gun tried to run after the bank robber.

    (A) spelled   (B) policed   (C) dated   (D) armed

_____ 2. I'm sorry that I picked up your phone by _____.

    (A) inch   (B) ant   (C) mistake   (D) lion

_____ 3. Peter is _____ of the dark, so he leaves a light on when he goes to bed.

    (A) quiet   (B) afraid   (C) noisy   (D) dangerous

_____ 4. Kelly took some medicine for the _____. She hoped it would ease the pain.

    (A) headache   (B) date   (C) king   (D) card

_____ 5. Your plan is only a _____ in the sky. You can never put it into practice.

    (A) lion   (B) king   (C) ant   (D) pie

Level 1 Test 26

Class: _____ No.: _____ Name: _____ Score: _____

I. 文意字彙 (40%)

_____ 1. It is traditional in Taiwan to eat mooncakes during the Mid-Autumn F_____ l.

_____ 2. Chien-Ming Wang was a famous b_____ l player.

_____ 3. Ted enjoys watching movies with a big bowl of buttered p_____ n.

_____ 4. Smelling something burning in the k_____ n, Mike ran to take a look.

_____ 5. Sam is a careful d_____ r for he always drives slowly and safely.

II. 字彙配合 (請忽略大小寫) (40%)

(A) stairs	(B) agreed	(C) notes	(D) bananas	(E) marked

_____ 1. Mr. Lee asked his students to take _____ in class.

_____ 2. Matthew _____ to sell his house to me at a very low price.

_____ 3. Hearing the doorbell ringing, Frankie ran down the _____ to open the door.

_____ 4. Bonnie _____ the important parts of the article with a red pen.

_____ 5. When people think of _____, they are likely to link them with monkeys.

III. 選擇題 (20%)

_____ 1. People can rent public _____ at a low price in this city.
   (A) stairs   (B) apples   (C) agreement   (D) bicycles

_____ 2. Edith is _____ of doing the same job over and over again.
   (A) orange   (B) sick   (C) dead   (D) pink

_____ 3. The soccer team practiced hard to _____ the game.
   (A) lose   (B) refuse   (C) win   (D) cry

_____ 4. To draw a straight line, you need to use a _____.
   (A) defeat   (B) cat   (C) pack   (D) ruler

_____ 5. Amy loved to watch cartoons when she was a little _____.
   (A) aunt   (B) kid   (C) hill   (D) soup

Level 1 Test 27

Class: _____ No.: _____ Name: _____ Score: _____

I. 文意字彙 (40%)

_____ 1. When the famous singer a_____ed at the airport, thousands of fans gathered there to welcome him.

_____ 2. To score goals, players have to throw the ball into the basket in a b_____l game.

_____ 3. For Jessie, spreading ugly rumors about people on the Internet is w_____g.

_____ 4. After careful consideration, Richard d_____ded to buy the red sports car.

_____ 5. Cathy lies all the time. Believe what she said is a s_____d thing to do.

II. 字彙配合 (請忽略大小寫) (40%)

(A) excited	(B) doll	(C) couch	(D) present	(E) sight

_____ 1. I don't have time at _____, but we can talk about it tonight.

_____ 2. Lie down and take a nap on the _____ if you feel sleepy.

_____ 3. Gina is _____ about the chance to study abroad.

_____ 4. It was romantic that Aiden and Millie fell in love with each other at first _____.

_____ 5. A(n) _____ is a small figure of a person that is used as a child's toy.

III. 選擇題 (20%)

_____ 1. On weekends, Howard goes to the _____ to do grocery shopping.
  (A) package   (B) supermarket   (C) item   (D) kiss

_____ 2. Frank didn't sleep well last night because of the loud _____ outside.
  (A) parcel   (B) vision   (C) noise   (D) bite

_____ 3. Smoking and drinking _____ to the loss of your health.
  (A) come   (B) pipe   (C) fill   (D) lead

_____ 4. Eunice ordered a mixed _____ for lunch, and her friend ordered a hamburger.
  (A) salad   (B) sound   (C) packet   (D) item

_____ 5. The teacher gave us a lot of homework; we had to read more than two hundred _____ in one day.
  (A) balls   (B) pages   (C) birds   (D) pools

Level 1 Test 28

Class: _____ No.: _____ Name: _____ Score: _____

I. 文意字彙 (40%)

_____ 1. I need a p_____r of scissors to cut this bag open.

_____ 2. The speaker cleared his t_____t before giving a speech.

_____ 3. The f_____y workers went on strike for better working conditions.

_____ 4. A leather j_____t can protect you against the freezing wind when you ride a scooter.

_____ 5. Could you turn down the TV, please? The baby is s_____ping.

II. 字彙配合 (請忽略大小寫) (40%)

(A) lucky	(B) blind	(C) cute	(D) busy	(E) sharp

_____ 1. Fiona is _____. She got the ticket to the popular singer's final show.

_____ 2. Be careful not to hurt yourself when you use these knives. They are very _____.

_____ 3. Tony liked the _____ design of that mug, so he bought it.

_____ 4. People who have this rare disease would go _____ slowly.

_____ 5. Mina and her team were _____ preparing for the trade fair.

III. 選擇題 (20%)

_____ 1. The boy has a real talent for art. He can _____ very well.

    (A) beach   (B) bat   (C) pot   (D) paint

_____ 2. Singers put out their albums in the form of _____ in the past.

    (A) bats   (B) bathtubs   (C) tapes   (D) ears

_____ 3. Dogs usually _____ themselves dry when they get wet.

    (A) die   (B) shake   (C) flower   (D) pot

_____ 4. Lisa went out to fly a _____ this afternoon because of the good weather.

    (A) bath   (B) beach   (C) ear   (D) kite

_____ 5. It's considered impolite to pick one's _____ in public.

    (A) nose   (B) bank   (C) bathtub   (D) flower

Level 1 Test 29

Class: _____ No.: _____ Name: _____ Score: _____

I. 文意字彙 (40%)

_____ 1. Be c_____l with the plates and cups. Don't break them.

_____ 2. From the mountaintop, the climber enjoyed a p_____y view over the valley.

_____ 3. Mr. Pearson's job is to milk the cows on a dairy f_____m.

_____ 4. I can't believe you finished a whole b_____e of beer within thirty seconds.

_____ 5. To keep healthy, we have to eat different fruit and v_____es.

II. 字彙配合 (請忽略大小寫) (40%)

(A) pond	(B) funny	(C) lamp	(D) dear	(E) bed

_____ 1. Raymond's brothers and sisters are very _____ to him.

_____ 2. In a youth hostel, nobody will make the _____ for you. You have to do it by yourself.

_____ 3. There are a lot of fish in the small _____ at the back of our house.

_____ 4. It is getting dark outside. Please turn on the table _____.

_____ 5. Ashley said something _____ and made her family laugh out loud.

III. 選擇題 (20%)

_____ 1. Monica shared the _____ of pasta and other dishes with her friends.

    (A) cab   (B) lamp   (C) dollar   (D) plate

_____ 2. Anna _____ two pieces of cloth together to make curtains.

    (A) pinned   (B) spoke   (C) emailed   (D) smiled

_____ 3. Andy was running late for work this morning, so he took a _____.

    (A) dollar   (B) post   (C) taxi   (D) pond

_____ 4. Little boys like to play _____ on little girls to get their attention.

    (A) potatoes   (B) jokes   (C) cabs   (D) shorts

_____ 5. You should study harder and then you can _____ up with your classmates.

    (A) smile   (B) mail   (C) speak   (D) catch

Level 1 Test 30

Class: _____ No.: _____ Name: _____ Score: _____

I. 文意字彙 (40%)

_____ 1. Don't forget to seal the e_____e before you mail it.

_____ 2. These scientists want to find another p_____t like the Earth in the universe.

_____ 3. The monster in the film looked very t_____e and scared many children.

_____ 4. The naughty boy took great p_____e in playing funny tricks on his classmates.

_____ 5. Employees of this company work very hard to make q_____k responses to customers' needs.

II. 字彙配合 (請忽略大小寫) (40%)

(A) video	(B) desk	(C) box	(D) map	(E) juice

_____ 1. Do you believe I can finish the whole _____ of chocolates at a time?

_____ 2. The tourists checked the _____ to make sure they were going in the right direction.

_____ 3. Tomato _____ is said to be able to help human body fight against certain diseases.

_____ 4. I'd rather watch a _____ of the movie at home than go to the theater.

_____ 5. After dinner, my father likes to sit at his _____, reading books.

III. 選擇題 (20%)

_____ 1. Victor invited some close _____ to join his birthday party.

    (A) clothes   (B) grandmothers   (C) lawyers   (D) friends

_____ 2. In most parts of Taiwan, it doesn't _____ in winter.

    (A) cook   (B) sack   (C) forget   (D) snow

_____ 3. When you cross the _____, it is important to look both ways.

    (A) bowl   (B) rabbit   (C) street   (D) fire

_____ 4. The baseball player hurt his _____. He couldn't bat or throw a ball.

    (A) bee   (B) rabbit   (C) shoulder   (D) bowl

_____ 5. The buildings in this area _____ to that private organization.

    (A) cook   (B) belong   (C) sack   (D) prepare

Level 1 Test 31

Class: _____ No.: _____ Name: _____ Score: _____

I. 文意字彙 (40%)

_____ 1. You have done a good job, and we are very p_____d of you.

_____ 2. Mr. Brown spent all day c_____ting his students' homework.

_____ 3. Allen was k_____ked out of school for his frequent misbehavior.

_____ 4. It was an exciting experience to r_____e on a roller coaster.

_____ 5. Working holiday programs allow people to stay in a f_____n country for one or two years.

II. 字彙配合 (請忽略大小寫) (40%)

(A) else	(B) twice	(C) pockets	(D) grade	(E) straight

_____ 1. To his disappointment, Tom only got a(n) _____ B in English.

_____ 2. Who _____ forgot to hand in the homework yesterday?

_____ 3. Ken went _____ to the bookstore after finishing his piano class.

_____ 4. Tiffany put her hands in the _____ to keep them warm.

_____ 5. Mandy goes to the gym _____ a week.

III. 選擇題 (20%)

_____ 1. Jay sat on the _____ and had his sandwich in the park.

(A) lip   (B) ticket   (C) butter   (D) bench

_____ 2. Mom baked an apple pie last _____.

(A) brown   (B) dictionary   (C) weekend   (D) grade

_____ 3. I prefer to eat with chopsticks rather than with a knife and _____.

(A) fork   (B) rainbow   (C) bell   (D) straight

_____ 4. Kids are only allowed to write in pencil, so they can rub out their errors with a(n) _____.

(A) eraser   (B) singer   (C) sir   (D) lip

_____ 5. It is necessary for you to develop a _____ of checking typing errors before sending emails.

(A) bell   (B) pocket   (C) habit   (D) gay

Level 1 Test 32

Class: _____ No.: _____ Name: _____ Score: _____

I. 文意字彙 (40%)

_____ 1. Would you mind opening the w_____w? It is quite hot here.

_____ 2. The f_____r had trouble communicating with the local people.

_____ 3. We c_____ed Robert's birthday by having dinner in the fast food restaurant together.

_____ 4. I didn't hear you. Could you r_____t your question?

_____ 5. It is dangerous to talk or text on a c_____e while driving.

II. 字彙配合 (請忽略大小寫) (40%)

(A) tidy	(B) hung	(C) slim	(D) blocked	(E) pulled

_____ 1. When his phone rang, the driver _____ over to answer it.

_____ 2. Since there was a march, the police _____ off the street from traffic.

_____ 3. The students are asked to keep their classroom _____.

_____ 4. The oil painting was _____ on the wall.

_____ 5. There is a _____ chance that Molly will win first prize in the song contest.

III. 選擇題 (20%)

_____ 1. The robber _____ out the guard to break into the bank and got away with a large sum of money.

    (A) hung   (B) knocked   (C) covered   (D) entered

_____ 2. Susan received a bunch of red _____ on her birthday.

    (A) roses   (B) parties   (C) queens   (D) series

_____ 3. Matt booked a three-star _____ for his business trip.

    (A) wife   (B) belt   (C) gift   (D) hotel

_____ 4. It was _____ of Pete to remember my birthday and send me a present.

    (A) mild   (B) slender   (C) sweet   (D) dirty

_____ 5. The coffee was too _____ to drink right away. You should wait before taking a sip.

    (A) neat   (B) messy   (C) lovely   (D) hot

Level 1 Test 33

Class: _____ No.: _____ Name: _____ Score: _____

I. 文意字彙 (40%)

_____ 1. Nobody answered the phone. P_____s all of them had left the office.

_____ 2. You are sure to make a good h_____d if you share household chores with your wife.

_____ 3. The r_____r arrived at the scene of the accident shortly after he received information.

_____ 4. After rubbing her t_____es, Victoria felt her headache getting better.

_____ 5. A s_____e has four corners and four straight sides of the same length.

II. 字彙配合 (請忽略大小寫) (40%)

(A) chair	(B) sat	(C) happened	(D) table	(E) worker

_____ 1. Marcus _____ on a tiny cottage when he was taking a walk in the woods.

_____ 2. The _____ fixed the broken machine with his tools.

_____ 3. If you are in the _____, you are the person in charge of a meeting or committee.

_____ 4. John _____ on the coach and read a magazine last night.

_____ 5. A lot of money had been passed under the _____ before the company obtained the contract.

III. 選擇題 (20%)

_____ 1. Please make sure to flush the _____ after use.

    (A) chicken   (B) mine   (C) toilet   (D) lemon

_____ 2. Nancy raised her hand and gave the correct _____ to the teacher's question.

    (A) boat   (B) answer   (C) fly   (D) rice

_____ 3. Landon _____ up as a Superman for the Halloween party.

    (A) dressed   (B) pulled   (C) chaired   (D) pushed

_____ 4. The class was so _____ that I fell asleep halfway through.

    (A) hungry   (B) crazy   (C) boring   (D) mad

_____ 5. I have told you _____ of times that you should knock before entering my room.

    (A) hundreds   (B) tables   (C) answers   (D) frogs

Level 1 Test 34

Class: _____ No.: _____ Name: _____ Score: _____

I. 文意字彙 (40%)

_____ 1. Nowadays, r_____ts are widely used to replace human workers.

_____ 2. It is said that the house is haunted by the g_____t of its original owner.

_____ 3. In Thailand, m_____ys are trained to climb trees to pick coconuts for human beings.

_____ 4. The movie star is too busy to answer l_____rs from his fans.

_____ 5. Greg dreams of being a software e_____r, so he learns quite a few computer programming languages.

II. 字彙配合 (請忽略大小寫) (40%)

| (A) dug | (B) strange | (C) threw | (D) borrowed | (E) thick |

_____ 1. The new job is _____ to me; I am not familiar with it at all.

_____ 2. Have you returned the book you _____ from the library?

_____ 3. The naughty girl _____ a stone at me and ran away.

_____ 4. It is impossible to see the oncoming cars through the _____ fog.

_____ 5. The rescue workers _____ through the rubble in search of other victims.

III. 選擇題 (20%)

_____ 1. To stay healthy, Jason decided to _____ the stair instead of taking the elevator.

    (A) pig   (B) club   (C) climb   (D) boss

_____ 2. As the sun set, the stars began to twinkle in the _____.

    (A) shirt   (B) giant   (C) quarter   (D) sky

_____ 3. Lucy is taking a bath in the _____.

    (A) jeans   (B) bathroom   (C) insect   (D) club

_____ 4. Gina got _____ after her husband passed away.

    (A) giant   (B) odd   (C) lonely   (D) dense

_____ 5. As I entered the classroom, Ian greeted me with a warm "_____."

    (A) hello   (B) dig   (C) hog   (D) quarter

Level 1 Test 35

Class: _____ No.: _____ Name: _____ Score: _____

I. 文意字彙 (40%)

_____ 1. If you can travel a_____d, what country would you like to go?

_____ 2. It could be a sign of illness if people l_____e weight rapidly.

_____ 3. The cake was c_____ted with frosting and melted chocolate.

_____ 4. This dictionary is very h_____l in learning Spanish.

_____ 5. Darren wiped his mouth with a paper t_____l after finishing his food.

II. 字彙配合 (請忽略大小寫) (40%)

(A) glad	(B) menu	(C) quiet	(D) tail	(E) bow

_____ 1. The teacher was _____ about the student's excellent performance.

_____ 2. The pianist gave a _____ to the audience and then started the concert.

_____ 3. We must keep _____ in the library so that we won't disturb others.

_____ 4. The _____ was written in French, so Rose didn't know what to order for dinner.

_____ 5. Seeing its master, the dog wagged its _____ excitedly.

III. 選擇題 (20%)

_____ 1. The _____ students avoided completing their report until the last minute.

(A) bottom (B) glad (C) comfortable (D) lazy

_____ 2. Ruby _____ her cow to the fence before heading into the farm.

(A) tied (B) rolled (C) won (D) jumped

_____ 3. We decided to go to the _____ to buy some food.

(A) snake (B) shop (C) toy (D) farmer

_____ 4. Tom carefully selected a pair of _____ for his long walk in the park.

(A) backsides (B) daughters (C) shoes (D) dozens

_____ 5. The boy yelled when he saw a deadly _____ in the grass.

(A) top (B) girl (C) store (D) snake

Level 1 Test 36

Class: _____ No.: _____ Name: _____ Score: _____

I. 文意字彙 (40%)

_____ 1. When did your hair start to turn g_____y? At the age of fifty or sixty?

_____ 2. Diane has been away from home for many years, and she m_____ses her family very much.

_____ 3. We depend on the r_____y season to bring us enough water to last for the whole year.

_____ 4. With proper medical t_____t, the patient recovered from his illness soon.

_____ 5. Please call me tomorrow morning if it is c_____t for you.

II. 字彙配合 (請忽略大小寫) (40%)

(A) dished	(B) month	(C) leader	(D) drew	(E) holiday

_____ 1. Kate planned to take a camping _____ with her family.

_____ 2. Jim was a natural _____. He guided our team with ease.

_____ 3. I'm excited about moving to New York next _____.

_____ 4. Mom _____ the cake out for me and my sister.

_____ 5. Miffy _____ a picture of her families during her art class.

III. 選擇題 (20%)

_____ 1. The song was a(n) _____ with teenagers immediately after it came out.
   (A) actress   (B) truck   (C) hit   (D) tie

_____ 2. Sometimes, a white _____ can avoid hurting one's feelings.
   (A) miss   (B) secretary   (C) spring   (D) lie

_____ 3. The eagles were _____ on chicken and other small animals.
   (A) fed   (B) lain   (C) collected   (D) drawn

_____ 4. Don't be afraid of Ben. He is just a paper _____.
   (A) son   (B) vacation   (C) tiger   (D) actor

_____ 5. Andrew had _____ in his stomach before he performed in front of the whole school.
   (A) butterflies   (B) leaders   (C) months   (D) springs

Level 1 Test 37

Class: _____ No.: _____ Name: _____ Score: _____

I. 文意字彙 (40%)

_____ 1. Your report is close to being perfect e_____t for one spelling error.

_____ 2. The doctor advised the patient to l_____n to soft music to calm himself down.

_____ 3. William gave his girlfriend a diamond r_____g and asked her to marry him.

_____ 4. Much to everyone's s_____e, the six-year-old boy won the race.

_____ 5. To be h_____t with you, I don't like the way you talk to me.

II. 字彙配合 (請忽略大小寫) (40%)

(A) cool	(B) finger	(C) stand	(D) wait	(E) lesson

_____ 1. David has sat at a computer for hours; he should _____ up and stretch.

_____ 2. Nelson learned a _____ from the foolish mistake he had made.

_____ 3. The children _____ for their father whenever he works overtime.

_____ 4. Never make any decision when you are mad. You had better _____ down first.

_____ 5. After the car accident, the passengers have pointed the _____ at the driver's carelessness.

III. 選擇題 (20%)

_____ 1. Before leaving the restaurant, Mia _____ the waiter for his good service.

(A) fingered (B) tipped (C) priced (D) waited

_____ 2. Evan was playing the electric _____ and singing his favorite song.

(A) guitar (B) button (C) brother (D) soldier

_____ 3. Wendy and her brother had beef noodles and corn soup for _____.

(A) cool (B) tennis (C) noon (D) dinner

_____ 4. Ivy wore a colorful _____ with a playful design to the outdoor event.

(A) stall (B) lesson (C) T-shirt (D) elephant

_____ 5. I enjoyed riding the _____ at the farm during the school field trip.

(A) stand (B) horse (C) midday (D) price

Level 1 Test 38

Class: _____ No.: _____ Name: _____ Score: _____

I. 文意字彙 (40%)

_____ 1. You cannot c____t on Kevin because he seldom keeps his word.

_____ 2. Molly is our Chinese teacher. She has been t____hing us for three years.

_____ 3. The weather was much colder than the campers had e____ted.

_____ 4. B____ns are seeds of plants which are often used as food.

_____ 5. I was s____d at Jimmy's reaction to the accident.

II. 字彙配合 (請忽略大小寫) (40%)

(A) mud	(B) root	(C) garden	(D) cake	(E) fan

_____ 1. The major function of the _____ of a plant is to get water and minerals from the soil.

_____ 2. Ben was the pop singer's big _____, so he was thrilled to see her in person.

_____ 3. There is a vegetable _____ behind the house, where peas and cabbages grow very well.

_____ 4. The chocolate _____ certainly goes well with the black coffee.

_____ 5. Your shoes are covered with dirty _____. Take them off before you enter the house.

III. 選擇題 (20%)

_____ 1. In order not to _____ the final exam, Ed studied very hard.
(A) fail (B) fan (C) hurt (D) join

_____ 2. Sandy turned on the _____ to listen to her favorite music while cooking dinner.
(A) wall (B) theater (C) star (D) radio

_____ 3. After a long day of work, Penny felt _____ and ready to relax at home.
(A) expensive (B) tired (C) cheap (D) married

_____ 4. Mom hung a beautiful painting on the _____ in her bedroom.
(A) wall (B) lunch (C) pants (D) guy

_____ 5. The basketball player gave a(n) _____ of joy when his team won the game.
(A) star (B) uncle (C) shout (D) cake

Level 1 Test 39

Class: _____ No.: _____ Name: _____ Score: _____

I. 文意字彙 (40%)

_____ 1. Bruce went to the house next door and asked his neighbor not to play l____d music.

_____ 2. Taking a cold s_____r on a hot day is very comfortable.

_____ 3. To make a bowl of salad, you can prepare some apples and t____oes.

_____ 4. I like to do my math problems in p_____l because it is easy to make corrections.

_____ 5. The m_____t the teacher entered the classroom, the students fell silent.

II. 字彙配合 (請忽略大小寫) (40%)

(A) joy	(B) rope	(C) ham	(D) fine	(E) gate

_____ 1. The driver got a NT$3,000 _____ for speeding on the highway.

_____ 2. The boatman used a _____ to fasten the boat to the pier.

_____ 3. I would like to have two slices of _____ and two eggs in my sandwich.

_____ 4. Betty's mother picks her up at the _____ after school every day.

_____ 5. Jane's life is filled with _____ after having the cute baby.

III. 選擇題 (20%)

_____ 1. Owen went to the police _____ to check on the progress of his stolen bicycle case.
   (A) cow   (B) welcome   (C) uniform   (D) station

_____ 2. Our bedrooms are located on the second _____ of the house.
   (A) beef   (B) circle   (C) floor   (D) height

_____ 3. Irene and I decided to _____ by the river and experience the beauty of nature.
   (A) camp   (B) fine   (C) total   (D) greet

_____ 4. The rock band is very popular with _____.
   (A) gates   (B) teenagers   (C) toes   (D) hams

_____ 5. We hope it doesn't _____ during our outdoor picnic tomorrow.
   (A) fine   (B) rain   (C) welcome   (D) total

Level 1 Test 40

Class: _____ No.: _____ Name: _____ Score: _____

I. 文意字彙 (40%)

_____ 1. Andy is neither at home nor in the office. M____e he is at his girlfriend's place.

_____ 2. Don't forget to set the alarm c____k, or you might be late for school.

_____ 3. I need some t____ls to fix the broken washing machine.

_____ 4. The t____e makes it possible for people to speak to the people in the distance.

_____ 5. The dictionary d____es a square as a rectangle with four equal sides.

II. 字彙配合 (請忽略大小寫) (40%)

(A) photographs	(B) sisters	(C) gloves	(D) wise	(E) sad

_____ 1. Tina wore a pair of _____ to protect her hands from the cold weather.

_____ 2. The little boy looked _____ when he realized he had lost his favorite toy.

_____ 3. The twin _____ celebrated their birthday together.

_____ 4. It is _____ of you to double-check the map before starting the drive.

_____ 5. Ken took lots of _____ of his children when they were playing at the beach.

III. 選擇題 (20%)

_____ 1. The little girl cried when her balloon was _____ away by the strong wind.
(A) roomed (B) thanked (C) blown (D) wished

_____ 2. Gary dropped to his _____ in the temple and began to say his prayers.
(A) meals (B) knees (C) nurses (D) carrots

_____ 3. Eva worked hard to _____ her homework before the deadline.
(A) call (B) photograph (C) notice (D) finish

_____ 4. Robert got very drunk and thus made a _____ of himself.
(A) violin (B) yes (C) tomorrow (D) fool

_____ 5. Lily and I _____ out of the theater and discussed our favorite scenes from the movie.
(A) walked (B) kneed (C) fooled (D) nursed

Level 2 Test 1

Class: _____ No.: _____ Name: _____ Score: _____

I. 文意字彙 (40%)

_____ 1. It is getting dark. T_____s, you had better go home soon.

_____ 2. Jamie didn't know what program she'd like to watch and kept changing c_____ls.

_____ 3. The f_____g example will give you a clear idea of how you can use your time more wisely.

_____ 4. I bought a table at a garage sale; this piece of f_____e cost me only twenty dollars.

_____ 5. Janet is good at making desserts, e_____y French desserts.

II. 字彙配合 (請忽略大小寫) (40%)

(A) nervous	(B) battle	(C) perfect	(D) sense	(E) quality

_____ 1. Roger gets lost easily because he has no _____ of direction.

_____ 2. Your writing is _____. I cannot find any mistake in it.

_____ 3. Sadly, thousands of soldiers lost their lives in _____.

_____ 4. The chef insists on using materials of the best _____ to prepare all the dishes.

_____ 5. Howard was _____ about speaking to a large audience, and he couldn't sleep well.

III. 選擇題 (20%)

_____ 1. Rita is always _____ to lend a helping hand to those in need.

    (A) rapid   (B) huge   (C) basic   (D) willing

_____ 2. The doctor _____ that Ken do more exercise to improve his health.

    (A) regressed   (B) suggested   (C) progressed   (D) directed

_____ 3. The roadwork in the downtown _____ has caused heavy traffic delays.

    (A) skin   (B) region   (C) bit   (D) progress

_____ 4. The new department store offers discounts to attract _____ during its first month.

    (A) customers   (B) bits   (C) areas   (D) means

_____ 5. This novel has a sad _____, and it makes many readers cry.

    (A) skin   (B) area   (C) ending   (D) china

Level 2

Level 2 Test 2

Class: _____ No.: _____ Name: _____ Score: _____

I. 文意字彙 (40%)

_____ 1. The natural beauty of the sunset was b____d description.

_____ 2. The restaurant served d_____s noodles with chicken soup and fresh vegetables.

_____ 3. Elliot studied hard for the exam; t____e, he was well-prepared and confident.

_____ 4. The railway system cost the government more than two b____n dollars to build.

_____ 5. The research shows that insects have a s____y with order.

II. 字彙配合 (請忽略大小寫) (40%)

(A) nor	(B) whenever	(C) such	(D) pleasant	(E) single

_____ 1. Lillian is _____ a sweet girl that everyone likes her a lot.

_____ 2. Ms. Johnson didn't get married and stayed _____ all her life.

_____ 3. If you don't go to the Christmas party, _____ will Jason and I.

_____ 4. Christopher is reading a crime novel _____ I visit him.

_____ 5. Gorge has a _____ personality, so he has many friends.

III. 選擇題 (20%)

_____ 1. Karen is Jill's friend on the _____; however, Karen often speaks ill of Jill behind her back.
　　(A) safety　　(B) field　　(C) puppy　　(D) surface

_____ 2. The old man took _____ in his son, who had just got a master's degree in law.
　　(A) pride　　(B) manager　　(C) safety　　(D) importance

_____ 3. The patient is getting well by _____, but it will be some time before he completely recovers.
　　(A) puppies　　(B) degrees　　(C) enemies　　(D) managers

_____ 4. The schedule of the boss _____ with the meeting time. The meeting time needs to be changed.
　　(A) gathers　　(B) behaves　　(C) conflicts　　(D) refuses

_____ 5. The only thing the homeless man owns is a(n) _____ to keep him warm at night.
　　(A) blanket　　(B) field　　(C) importance　　(D) safety

Level 2 Test 3

Class: _____ No.: _____ Name: _____ Score: _____

I. 文意字彙 (40%)

_____ 1. Sue wants to apply to a u_____y after she finishes senior high school.

_____ 2. Ed is g_____s with his money and willing to help people.

_____ 3. Andrew didn't r_____e the value of health until he lost it.

_____ 4. Victor and Ivy's m_____e didn't work out well ; they got a divorce.

_____ 5. Nancy looked upset. It was o_____s that she was not satisfied with our decision.

II. 字彙配合 (請忽略大小寫) (40%)

(A) direct   (B) usual   (C) symbol   (D) particular   (E) favor

_____ 1. The illness has made Zack weak. He doesn't seem his _____ self anymore.

_____ 2. Stephen King is one of my favorite writers, and I enjoy his latest novel in _____.

_____ 3. Because of its commercial value, the local people are in _____ of building a shopping mall.

_____ 4. The teacher maintains _____ contact with parents to let them know their child's progress in school.

_____ 5. The rainbow in the poem is a _____ of a promising future.

III. 選擇題 (20%)

_____ 1. Mrs. Lee had to change her work _____ to take care of her sick son.

     (A) cause   (B) schedule   (C) government   (D) diamond

_____ 2. The tennis player didn't expect to win. It happened entirely by _____.

     (A) accident   (B) diet   (C) timetable   (D) border

_____ 3. We will _____ the party to celebrate our friend's birthday.

     (A) border   (B) include   (C) attend   (D) challenge

_____ 4. In our company, we _____ safety as an important issue for all employees.

     (A) cause   (B) diet   (C) include   (D) regard

_____ 5. It's necessary to pay the _____ on time to avoid any late fees.

     (A) timetable   (B) government   (C) bill   (D) challenge

Level 2

Level 2 Test 4

Class: _____ No.: _____ Name: _____ Score: _____

I. 文意字彙 (40%)

_____ 1. Mia c_____med to have finished the report, but her teacher didn't believe her.

_____ 2. The s_____e woman is easily angered by other people's words.

_____ 3. Everyone should be treated equally, regardless of race or r_____n.

_____ 4. Although Mr. Lin is 84, he still has an a_____e social life.

_____ 5. The United States is believed to be one of the most powerful n_____ns in the world.

II. 字彙配合 (請忽略大小寫) (40%)

(A) prize	(B) tradition	(C) sex	(D) purpose	(E) instance

_____ 1. With modern technology, we can know the _____ of a baby before it is born.

_____ 2. Don't be too hard on the boy. He didn't break the window on _____.

_____ 3. Henry was given a(n) _____ for winning the swimming race.

_____ 4. Grace is very lazy; for _____, she doesn't even wash dishes or do her laundry.

_____ 5. It is a _____ for Chinese people to give children red envelopes on Chinese New Year's eve.

III. 選擇題 (20%)

_____ 1. The patient keeps a _____ record of the medicine he takes every day.

    (A) main   (B) final   (C) average   (D) daily

_____ 2. Can you give me _____ to the nearest gas station?

    (A) directions   (B) bases   (C) oceans   (D) brands

_____ 3. The popular singer's _____ dates for the concert will soon be announced.

    (A) average   (B) primary   (C) brilliant   (D) official

_____ 4. A _____ of a dictionary is to provide definitions and meanings for words.

    (A) final   (B) function   (C) glue   (D) ease

_____ 5. Understanding the _____ between regular exercise and good health is important for maintaining a healthy lifestyle.

    (A) bottom   (B) ease   (C) relationship   (D) brand

Level 2 Test 5

Class: _____ No.: _____ Name: _____ Score: _____

I. 文意字彙 (40%)

_____ 1. Only a baby had a narrow e_____e from the accident; all the other passengers got killed.

_____ 2. With the a_____s, I believe I can find Jacob's house.

_____ 3. Our teacher always e_____es the importance of practicing speaking English every day.

_____ 4. The first public library in the United States was f_____ded by Benjamin Franklin.

_____ 5. The president showed up at the event under g_____d.

II. 字彙配合 (請忽略大小寫) (40%)

(A) network	(B) major	(C) commercial	(D) style	(E) private

_____ 1. Does the discovery have any _____ value? Can we make money out of it?

_____ 2. Although Oscar seems friendly in public, he gets angry easily in _____.

_____ 3. The city has a good _____ of subways, which enables people to get around easily.

_____ 4. Most parents' _____ concern is whether their children can grow up safely.

_____ 5. Some people think that miniskirts are out of _____ now.

III. 選擇題 (20%)

_____ 1. As the storm approached, the experienced climber decided to _____ shelter.

    (A) calm   (B) seek   (C) stress   (D) frighten

_____ 2. May's strong _____ in God helped her overcome the challenges she faced.

    (A) peak   (B) shelf   (C) coast   (D) belief

_____ 3. The tourist _____ in the towns near the sea has grown over the past few years.

    (A) industry   (B) scare   (C) deer   (D) beauty

_____ 4. After a long day at work, Paul was not tired. He was still full of _____.

    (A) coast   (B) peak   (C) energy   (D) calm

_____ 5. After a discussion, Mike and his friends decided to _____ this area by train instead of driving themselves.

    (A) receive   (B) establish   (C) fix   (D) travel

Level 2

Level 2 Test 6

Class: _____ No.: _____ Name: _____ Score: _____

I. 文意字彙 (40%)

_____ 1. The little girl was e_____ed to try again after falling off her bike.

_____ 2. The Red Cross is an o_____n that aims to help people in need.

_____ 3. Mr. Jackson was seriously ill and needed to get some m_____l treatments immediately.

_____ 4. I don't know how to operate such a c_____x machine. Could you give me a hand?

_____ 5. Hailey planned to spend a c_____e of days in New York City.

II. 字彙配合 (請忽略大小寫) (40%)

(A) seldom	(B) weight	(C) flight	(D) instead	(E) memory

_____ 1. Chinese people have a dragon boat race every year in _____ of a poet, Qu Yuan.

_____ 2. Tiffany has _____ met her sisters since she left home and went to university.

_____ 3. It is unbelievable that the newborn baby is nearly five kilograms in _____.

_____ 4. Irena was attracted to the birds in _____ when she drove along the coast.

_____ 5. Nelson hung out with his friends _____ of doing his homework.

III. 選擇題 (20%)

_____ 1. The _____ showed great skills on the football field and scored a crucial goal for the team.
    (A) pose   (B) forward   (C) century   (D) trouble

_____ 2. The country attracted foreign _____ through investment opportunities and economic policies.
    (A) bother   (B) saw   (C) male   (D) capital

_____ 3. Nina successfully found a quick and effective solution to _____ the problem.
    (A) handle   (B) certain   (C) resume   (D) seem

_____ 4. After a discussion, the team _____ a new plan so as to finish the project in limited time.
    (A) sawed   (B) bothered   (C) proposed   (D) shot

_____ 5. It's wise to take _____ from experienced people when making decisions.
    (A) pose   (B) century   (C) female   (D) advice

Level 2 Test 7

Class: _____ No.: _____ Name: _____ Score: _____

I. 文意字彙 (40%)

_____ 1. Small talk is a good way to start a c_____n with strangers.

_____ 2. You have to pay e_____a money for the bread. It is not included in the meal.

_____ 3. Before the exam, the teacher reminded us to a_____d making the same mistakes.

_____ 4. The loving mother always g_____ts her children back from school at the door.

_____ 5. In a_____t times, people recorded events by drawing pictures.

II. 字彙配合 (請忽略大小寫) (40%)

(A) force	(B) possibility	(C) danger	(D) painting	(E) origin

_____ 1. The little boy opened the heavy door with all his _____.

_____ 2. An art collector bought the _____ of the famous artist with millions of dollars.

_____ 3. Dennis often gets hurt, for he doesn't pay attention to the _____ around him.

_____ 4. Is there any _____ for a human being to live to 200 years old?

_____ 5. The custom has been passed down for centuries, so it is hard to find its _____.

III. 選擇題 (20%)

_____ 1. Jessica is very shy and has _____ in speaking in public.

    (A) difficulty   (B) material   (C) similarity   (D) chain

_____ 2. To give his kids _____ rooms, Mr. White moved to a bigger house.

    (A) likely   (B) silent   (C) separate   (D) abnormal

_____ 3. The train arrives at the station at _____ intervals throughout the day.

    (A) regular   (B) modern   (C) alive   (D) natural

_____ 4. Understanding the _____ between these two ideas is crucial for effective decision-making.

    (A) role   (B) fabric   (C) speaker   (D) difference

_____ 5. Claudia is in _____ of organizing the event. She makes sure everything runs properly.

    (A) chain   (B) charge   (C) role   (D) typhoon

Level 2

Level 2 Test 8

Class: _____ No.: _____ Name: _____ Score: _____

I. 文意字彙 (40%)

_____ 1. Richard got the high-paying job because of his good e_____n and work experience.

_____ 2. Could you d_____e in detail what your attacker looked like?

_____ 3. The p_____n in that country is increasing so rapidly that there won't be enough food soon.

_____ 4. After years of discussion, the two nations finally decided to make p_____e with each other.

_____ 5. Visit our website for f_____r information about the event.

II. 字彙配合 (請忽略大小寫) (40%)

(A) prove	(B) shot	(C) instant	(D) return	(E) switch

_____ 1. The police found that the man was killed by a(n) _____ in the chest.

_____ 2. When I saw the smoke in the kitchen, I knew in a(n) _____ that something was wrong.

_____ 3. This gym offers good deals to customers who _____ over from other gyms.

_____ 4. Sandy helped the old man carry his heavy bag. In _____, he gave her a book.

_____ 5. The lawyer worked hard to _____ her client's innocence in the courtroom.

III. 選擇題 (20%)

_____ 1. The witness recognized the suspect based on her special physical _____.
(A) pop (B) success (C) appearance (D) crowd

_____ 2. Jason is the kindest person I have ever met in my _____ life.
(A) comic (B) entire (C) wild (D) chief

_____ 3. The musician is a leading _____ in the jazz community. People respect him for his talent and influence.
(A) figure (B) change (C) discovery (D) failure

_____ 4. Carl worked hard to become financially _____. He also managed his expenses and investments wisely.
(A) comic (B) pop (C) chief (D) independent

_____ 5. With a fresh coat of paint, the surface of this wooden table becomes pretty _____.
(A) whole (B) tragic (C) smooth (D) wild

Level 2 Test 9

Class: _____ No.: _____ Name: _____ Score: _____

I. 文意字彙 (40%)

_____ 1. You have to show your i_____y card to prove that you are over 18 before you get into a pub.

_____ 2. These police officers worked around the clock to s_____e the crime and brought the killer to justice.

_____ 3. The young kid is good at playing such musical i_____ts as the violin and the piano.

_____ 4. Grace p_____rs in-store shopping because she likes to see and touch the fabric.

_____ 5. Sandy's grandfather died from liver c_____r last year.

II. 字彙配合 (請忽略大小寫) (40%)

(A) similar	(B) focus	(C) display	(D) confident	(E) classical

_____ 1. Bach and Mozart are two of my favorite _____ composers.

_____ 2. The select shop had an eye-catching window _____. It presented the latest fashion trends.

_____ 3. The two paintings are so _____ that we cannot tell one from the other.

_____ 4. Unfortunately, the photo was out of _____. Its details were not clear.

_____ 5. Encouragement can help students become more _____ about themselves.

III. 選擇題 (20%)

_____ 1. Nelson joined the _____ and became a soldier at the age of 20.

    (A) decline   (B) goal   (C) dot   (D) army

_____ 2. We start using green products that don't damage the _____.

    (A) environment   (B) value   (C) football   (D) growth

_____ 3. The article described the _____ economic situation. It pointed out both challenges and opportunities for growth recently.

    (A) human   (B) royal   (C) current   (D) firm

_____ 4. Bobby carefully packed his _____ belongings before he moved out.

    (A) different   (B) personal   (C) human   (D) royal

_____ 5. Teddy reads the _____ carefully so as to use the copy machine correctly.

    (A) targets   (B) realities   (C) coins   (D) instructions

Level 2

Level 2 Test 10

Class: _____ No.: _____ Name: _____ Score: _____

I. 文意字彙 (40%)

_____ 1. The big computer company d_____ped from an office with only two programmers.

_____ 2. The government advised farmers to use as few c_____ls as possible on their crops.

_____ 3. Jimmy is the f____r drummer of this band. He quits the band and works at the bank now.

_____ 4. From Rachel's facial e_____n, we can know that she is sad.

_____ 5. The i_____n of tomatoes to Europe can be traced back to the 16th century.

II. 字彙配合 (請忽略大小寫) (40%)

(A) support	(B) favorite	(C) iron	(D) recover	(E) proper

_____ 1. With rest and medication, you will soon _____ from the flu.

_____ 2. The single father took two jobs to _____ his four children.

_____ 3. You'd better _____ your suit before going for the job interview.

_____ 4. Of the seven days in a week, my _____ day is Saturday.

_____ 5. It is not _____ to dress in red when you go to a funeral.

III. 選擇題 (20%)

_____ 1. Mr. Webber had a bad backache, so he took some aspirins to kill the _____.

(A) peace   (B) pain   (C) fit   (D) sand

_____ 2. Andy's desire to learn had a positive _____ on his performance at school.

(A) effect   (B) link   (C) judge   (D) war

_____ 3. Buying expensive tools that you don't use can be a _____ of money.

(A) childhood   (B) tax   (C) waste   (D) spirit

_____ 4. Natalie set a strict time _____ for her work to keep the balance between her professional and personal life.

(A) press   (B) production   (C) link   (D) limit

_____ 5. The _____ between Janet's studies and personal interest in human history led her to become a historian.

(A) connection   (B) judge   (C) spelling   (D) command

Level 2 Test 11

Class: _____ No.: _____ Name: _____ Score: _____

I. 文意字彙 (40%)

_____ 1. The workers in the chemical factory are required to wear protective c_____g.

_____ 2. Trust me! The news came from a reliable s_____e.

_____ 3. You are still young. Why don't you seize the g_____n opportunity to study abroad?

_____ 4. Repeated failures have resulted in Linda's l_____s of courage.

_____ 5. Going to the movies is Kevin's favorite leisure a_____y.

II. 字彙配合 (請忽略大小寫) (40%)

(A) throughout	(B) stick	(C) against	(D) gain	(E) express

_____ 1. Our team will play _____ a tough opponent in the next match.

_____ 2. It's difficult for the foreign student to _____ himself in Chinese.

_____ 3. The song is popular _____ the world. Almost everyone knows it.

_____ 4. If we want to handle these problems, we should _____ together.

_____ 5. Before you start a full-time job, it's better _____ experience from internships or part-time work.

III. 選擇題 (20%)

_____ 1. I am _____ of hungry. Would you like to eat out with me?

    (A) job   (B) folk   (C) snack   (D) sort

_____ 2. The man was determined to turn over a new _____ after being released from prison.

    (A) delivery   (B) leaf   (C) type   (D) spider

_____ 3. Mark is _____ for the project. He needs to make sure its success.

    (A) whole   (B) responsible   (C) recent   (D) total

_____ 4. The actress is always on a diet for _____ of being out of shape.

    (A) fear   (B) task   (C) kind   (D) toothbrush

_____ 5. The students raised questions. It showed they were _____ about the topic being discussed in class.

    (A) mature   (B) latest   (C) curious   (D) complete

Level 2

Level 2 Test 12

Class: _____ No.: _____ Name: _____ Score: _____

I. 文意字彙 (40%)

_____ 1. The rescue team was excited. They d_____red that several earthquake victims were still alive.

_____ 2. In g_____l, the summer weather in Taiwan is hot and humid.

_____ 3. At 82 years old, May lives a_____e in the city. She enjoys her independence.

_____ 4. Germany is famous for its great advances in science and t_____y.

_____ 5. Anna m_____ed the width of the available space in the room before she bought the sofa.

II. 字彙配合 (請忽略大小寫) (40%)

(A) building	(B) period	(C) president	(D) cycle	(E) college

_____ 1. Taipei 101 was once the tallest _____ in the world.

_____ 2. After you graduate from high school, you can go to _____.

_____ 3. I think the _____ of the seasons is nature's amazing work.

_____ 4. The _____ of a democratic country is elected by its people.

_____ 5. After a short _____ of embarrassing silence, the boy finally began to talk.

III. 選擇題 (20%)

_____ 1. The farmer wears _____ boots when working to prevent his feet from getting wet.

    (A) form   (B) bike   (C) rubber   (D) unit

_____ 2. Even though Dr. Shepherd is an excellent scientist, he remains _____.

    (A) gold   (B) humble   (C) southern   (D) typical

_____ 3. The owner had the house repaired. He wanted to keep it in good _____.

    (A) form   (B) university   (C) giraffe   (D) condition

_____ 4. Charlie is looking for clothes that are _____ for the special occasion.

    (A) suitable   (B) former   (C) liberal   (D) proud

_____ 5. Politeness and friendly manner are _____ when you communicate with people.

    (A) latter   (B) necessary   (C) typical   (D) gold

Level 2 Test 13

Class: _____ No.: _____ Name: _____ Score: _____

I. 文意字彙 (40%)

_____ 1. Shel Silverstein was c_____red one of the most important poets of the 20th century.

_____ 2. There are high mountains in the c_____l part of Taiwan.

_____ 3. It is going to be dark. We had b_____r go home right away.

_____ 4. According to the Bible, God created the u_____e.

_____ 5. As to the problem, do you have a better s_____n?

II. 字彙配合 (請忽略大小寫) (40%)

(A) downloaded	(B) thought	(C) amounted	(D) distance	(E) length

_____ 1. Louis kept his _____ from Andy after finding that he was a dishonest person.

_____ 2. The losses caused by the typhoon _____ to 50 million NT dollars.

_____ 3. After Jim gave _____ to the job offer, he decided to accept it.

_____ 4. The salesman went on at great _____ about the new coffee machine.

_____ 5. Landon illegally _____ some pop music from the music website.

III. 選擇題 (20%)

_____ 1. During the graduation ceremony, the speaker _____ an encouraging speech to inspire the graduating students.

(A) guided   (B) provided   (C) steeled   (D) delivered

_____ 2. When you see a word you don't know, looking up its _____ in a dictionary is helpful.

(A) meaning   (B) project   (C) wood   (D) idea

_____ 3. The former police officer began to write detective _____ after he left the job.

(A) hosts   (B) individuals   (C) novels   (D) metals

_____ 4. Tom had a stomachache, so he ate much less than _____.

(A) excellent   (B) usual   (C) perfect   (D) super

_____ 5. Connie believes in the power of _____ thinking. She thinks it helps her deal with difficulty.

(A) negative   (B) worse   (C) metal   (D) positive

Level 2

Level 2 Test 14

Class: _____ No.: _____ Name: _____ Score: _____

I. 文意字彙 (40%)

_____ 1. As the typhoon is a_____hing, you'd better make sure the shop sign is fastened.

_____ 2. There are c_____l differences even in the same country such as different beliefs and body language.

_____ 3. I cannot a_____t the present because it is too expensive.

_____ 4. TV programs have an i_____e on children's behavior.

_____ 5. In my o_____n, you should take a day off and get some rest.

II. 字彙配合 (請忽略大小寫) (40%)

(A) method	(B) survival	(C) climate	(D) record	(E) youth

_____ 1. The talented swimmer broke the _____ and won a gold medal.

_____ 2. Wow! You look so great. Can you tell me the secret of keeping your _____?

_____ 3. Generally speaking, the _____ in Taiwan is hot and humid.

_____ 4. The woman's _____ in the plane crash was a miracle of God.

_____ 5. We are encouraged to find out the most efficient _____ of doing our work.

III. 選擇題 (20%)

_____ 1. The medical team developed a new and _____ treatment to fight this disease.

(A) whole　　(B) western　　(C) effective　　(D) historical

_____ 2. Felix grew up with smartphones and the Internet. He can't _____ life without them.

(A) imagine　　(B) master　　(C) refuse　　(D) sport

_____ 3. After a discussion, the judges has made the _____ and will announce the winner later.

(A) good　　(B) mail　　(C) blood　　(D) decision

_____ 4. If you want to know the location of the toy _____, you can look at the floor map.

(A) department　　(B) master　　(C) evil　　(D) mail

_____ 5. When you are tired and under _____, you make mistakes more easily.

(A) position　　(B) post　　(C) stress　　(D) liquid

Level 2 Test 15

Class: _____ No.: _____ Name: _____ Score: _____

I. 文意字彙 (40%)

_____ 1. It is not l_____l to sell alcoholic drinks to people under 18.

_____ 2. Our teacher set a high s_____d for us. He wanted all of us to pass the exam.

_____ 3. This is an i_____l airport. All staff here can speak more than one language.

_____ 4. E_____l pollution is worsening with the rapid development of heavy industry.

_____ 5. Many book reviewers speak h_____y of the writer's latest novel. Therefore, it sells very well.

II. 字彙配合 (請忽略大小寫) (40%)

(A) image	(B) existence	(C) effort	(D) advance	(E) account

_____ 1. The restaurant is very popular; I suggest you make a reservation in _____.

_____ 2. Oliver looks a lot like his father; that is, he is the living _____ of his father.

_____ 3. Students must on no _____ use smartphones in the classroom without a teacher's permission.

_____ 4. It is said that the custom has been in _____ for a very long time.

_____ 5. Frank wrote a love letter to Carrie in a(n) _____ to win her heart.

III. 選擇題 (20%)

_____ 1. Headaches and loss of sleep are the signs people may experience when they are under great _____.

(A) pressure (B) teen (C) mate (D) data

_____ 2. The kind restaurant owner _____ up delicious food at a cheap price.

(A) improves (B) creates (C) manages (D) serves

_____ 3. The nurse took my _____ and told me I had a fever.

(A) negative (B) temperature (C) phrase (D) musician

_____ 4. The mysterious new _____ is fatal and spreads very quickly.

(A) phrase (B) mate (C) disease (D) data

_____ 5. Mia is interested in making films. She wants to become a movie _____.

(A) negative (B) teen (C) musician (D) director

Level 2 Test 16

Class: _____ No.: _____ Name: _____ Score: _____

I. 文意字彙 (40%)

_____ 1. This white wine from France is better than that one in t_____ms of quality.

_____ 2. Since I don't know much about Tom, I am in no p_____n to say anything about him.

_____ 3. Airplanes and hot-air balloons are both a_____t.

_____ 4. The number of electric scooters around the world is on the i_____e as more people care about the environment.

_____ 5. The police thought that there might be some l_____ks between the two cases.

II. 字彙配合 (請忽略大小寫) (40%)

(A) speech	(B) affected	(C) nail	(D) melody	(E) disappear

_____ 1. The morning fog began to _____ as the sun rose higher in the sky.

_____ 2. Teenagers are easily _____ by their friends and classmates.

_____ 3. Bobby hit his finger when he was trying to drive a(n) _____ into the wall.

_____ 4. The principal made a(n) _____ to all the students in the school gym.

_____ 5. When Paula is happy, she has a habit of singing the _____ of her favorite song.

III. 選擇題 (20%)

_____ 1. Mr. White is a(n) _____ on butterflies.
   (A) factor　　(B) expert　　(C) nail　　(D) user

_____ 2. It is _____ that everyone gets a chance to express their opinions.
   (A) fair　　(B) wooden　　(C) female　　(D) inexpert

_____ 3. Bob _____ on a sharp stone and hurt his foot.
   (A) connected　　(B) affected　　(C) stepped　　(D) titled

_____ 4. This restaurant is the best place to try _____ dishes.
   (A) patient　　(B) minor　　(C) local　　(D) unfair

_____ 5. My boyfriend was sent to _____ for attacking a police officer.
   (A) male　　(B) attention　　(C) decrease　　(D) prison

Level 2 Test 17

Class: _____ No.: _____ Name: _____ Score: _____

I. 文意字彙 (40%)

_____ 1. *West Side Story* is a well-known m_____l.

_____ 2. Sadly, only one person s_____ed the terrible accident.

_____ 3. Rick wanted to t_____e his chocolate cake for Jerry's new toy.

_____ 4. All the plants and flowers in the garden died for l_____k of water.

_____ 5. The next step is to add some sugar to the m_____e of eggs and milk.

II. 字彙配合 (請忽略大小寫) (40%)

(A) anger	(B) match	(C) alarm	(D) author	(E) feature

_____ 1. On hearing the gunshot, all the animals ran away in _____.

_____ 2. The players felt sad when they lost the football _____.

_____ 3. The _____ of the novel used his pen name instead of his real name.

_____ 4. Burning with _____, Sam's girlfriend said she was going to break up with him.

_____ 5. This large library is the main _____ of the city.

III. 選擇題 (20%)

_____ 1. The actor is _____ to play the role of a cowboy in his next movie.

    (A) powerful   (B) nearby   (C) common   (D) due

_____ 2. The president clearly _____ her thoughts on what would be best for the country.

    (A) featured   (B) stated   (C) toured   (D) swapped

_____ 3. The race car is moving at a(n) _____ of eighty miles per hour.

    (A) speed   (B) match   (C) shortage   (D) author

_____ 4. Ms. Lin is on _____ in Thailand right now. Would you like to leave a message?

    (A) alarm   (B) failure   (C) vacation   (D) anger

_____ 5. Receiving the news about my grandfather's death filled me with a _____ of sadness.

    (A) writer   (B) system   (C) success   (D) feeling

Level 2

Level 2 Test 18

Class: _____ No.: _____ Name: _____ Score: _____

I. 文意字彙 (40%)

_____ 1. Frank's parents strongly o_____ted to his leaving school to find a job.

_____ 2. In a_____n to water, the country is also short of food.

_____ 3. The valley of Loire in France p_____es some of the best wines in the world.

_____ 4. The teacher a_____ted to introduce a new teaching method, but the principal disagreed.

_____ 5. Long skirts are in f_____n now. Almost every young girl on the streets wears one.

II. 字彙配合 (請忽略大小寫) (40%)

(A) flat	(B) protect	(C) require	(D) military	(E) remove

_____ 1. If you _____ more details about our company, please contact me.

_____ 2. You should put on a hat to _____ your head from the heat.

_____ 3. Mr. Hill got a _____ tire on his way home and needed roadside assistance.

_____ 4. Harper tried very hard to _____ the dirty spots from his shirt.

_____ 5. John became very strong after completing two years of _____ service.

III. 選擇題 (20%)

_____ 1. We went for a hike in the _____ and enjoyed the sounds of nature.

    (A) discussion   (B) forest   (C) rubbish   (D) apartment

_____ 2. Sarah received a(n) _____ necklace as a wedding gift from her grandmother.

    (A) asleep   (B) flat   (C) valuable   (D) military

_____ 3. It is common for earthquakes to _____ in regions around the Pacific Ocean.

    (A) operate   (B) protect   (C) distrust   (D) occur

_____ 4. High winds caused the fire to _____ rapidly through the dry grass.

    (A) spread   (B) produce   (C) remove   (D) require

_____ 5. The _____ during the town hall meeting covered many important topics.

    (A) waist   (B) discussion   (C) trash   (D) trust

Level 2 Test 19

Class: _____ No.: _____ Name: _____ Score: _____

I. 文意字彙 (40%)

_____ 1. Aaron was born and raised in Canada, and no w____r he can speak English so well.

_____ 2. Natalie chose to stay at home r____r than go out on a rainy day.

_____ 3. In the eighteenth century, many people went to California in s____h of gold.

_____ 4. There is a little church on the e____e of the forest.

_____ 5. Mr. Jackson went to see a doctor in the c____y of his wife.

II. 字彙配合 (請忽略大小寫) (40%)

(A) participate	(B) contact	(C) balance	(D) range	(E) owner

_____ 1. I have a cousin, but I lost _____ with him many years ago.

_____ 2. If you want to do the part-time job, you'd better strike a(n) _____ between work and study.

_____ 3. The teacher encouraged her students to actively _____ in the class discussion.

_____ 4. The ages of the students in the summer camp _____ from 12 to 17.

_____ 5. We were invited by the _____ of the house to attend his dinner party.

III. 選擇題 (20%)

_____ 1. Bill got the _____, so he didn't go to school yesterday.
　　(A) flu 　　(B) contact 　　(C) rock 　　(D) balance

_____ 2. It's quite common for dogs to _____ at strangers.
　　(A) range 　　(B) participate 　　(C) offer 　　(D) bark

_____ 3. Learning a new language is considered good for the _____.
　　(A) court 　　(B) brain 　　(C) owner 　　(D) imbalance

_____ 4. The houses in this small village are built of _____.
　　(A) mass 　　(B) agreement 　　(C) stone 　　(D) awe

_____ 5. During the _____ meeting, people discussed important business matters.
　　(A) lower 　　(B) neither 　　(C) formal 　　(D) whatever

Level 2 Test 20

Class: _____ No.: _____ Name: _____ Score: _____

I. 文意字彙 (40%)

_____ 1. The car suddenly went out of c____l and hit the wall.

_____ 2. The typhoon caused serious d____e to several cities in the country.

_____ 3. We were forced to stay here for another day as a r____t of heavy snow.

_____ 4. Children should show r____t for their parents and teachers.

_____ 5. There aren't any seats a____e for tonight's show.

II. 字彙配合 (請忽略大小寫) (40%)

(A) basis	(B) model	(C) article	(D) crisis	(E) goal

_____ 1. Did you read the _____ on education in today's newspaper?

_____ 2. I firmly believe that Patrick will realize his _____ in the future.

_____ 3. We review our progress on a monthly _____ to see if we can do better.

_____ 4. Some companies couldn't survive the debt _____ and closed down.

_____ 5. To be a fashion _____, Meghan exercises every day to keep slim.

III. 選擇題 (20%)

_____ 1. It is not easy for some people to hide their _____, as their faces often show their true feelings.

    (A) items   (B) emotions   (C) articles   (D) plains

_____ 2. Emily trusted me very much and let me know about her _____ plan.

    (A) secret   (B) simple   (C) worse   (D) obvious

_____ 3. Mary is expected to give _____ to her first child in the coming month.

    (A) basis   (B) soccer   (C) cash   (D) birth

_____ 4. Children in the _____ often played together in the central square.

    (A) message   (B) personality   (C) village   (D) model

_____ 5. We are planning to _____ a new menu that is both healthy and delicious.

    (A) stage   (B) supply   (C) pattern   (D) design

Level 2 Test 21

Class: _____ No.: _____ Name: _____ Score: _____

I. 文意字彙 (40%)

_____ 1. Tucker had to take care of everything during his boss's a_____e.

_____ 2. I wrote to Mina often, but she never r_____lied to my letters.

_____ 3. Georgia is hard to please; it seems that nothing can s_____y her.

_____ 4. The novel is really great, and it is w_____h reading.

_____ 5. Garry moved to another city because he couldn't pay the r_____t here.

II. 字彙配合 (請忽略大小寫) (40%)

(A) edition	(B) truth	(C) corn	(D) gun	(E) blackboard

_____ 1. The hunter aimed his _____ at the deer but missed it.

_____ 2. The restaurant offers _____ soup and tomato soup for customers to choose from.

_____ 3. If Hank had told his mother the _____, she would not have been so angry.

_____ 4. The school chose the new _____ of the textbook, for it was more interesting.

_____ 5. The teacher asked her students to take down whatever she wrote on the _____.

III. 選擇題 (20%)

_____ 1. The bridge is so _____ that we cannot cross it at the same time.

    (A) eastern   (B) electric   (C) narrow   (D) rocky

_____ 2. The hotel was very good, and every _____ had a comfortable stay during their visit.

    (A) guest   (B) edition   (C) camel   (D) freedom

_____ 3. Sarah likes to _____ different fruits together to make a sweet salad.

    (A) answer   (B) mix   (C) gun   (D) let

_____ 4. Remember to wash your hands with _____ and water after touching dirty things.

    (A) truth   (B) toothache   (C) soap   (D) corn

_____ 5. Mia is a good _____, always paying attention to what others have to say.

    (A) papaya   (B) listener   (C) blackboard   (D) subway

Level 2

Level 2 Test 22

Class: _____ No.: _____ Name: _____ Score: _____

I. 文意字彙 (40%)

_____ 1. My friend, Brian, is good at playing b____n and tennis.

_____ 2. Caught in a t____p, the dog cried in pain.

_____ 3. The selfish boy has difficulty forming lasting f____ps with his classmates.

_____ 4. For safety concerns, it is better to change the p____d to your mailbox regularly.

_____ 5. We need to repair those e____l appliances as soon as possible.

II. 字彙配合 (請忽略大小寫) (40%)

(A) motion	(B) responded	(C) aid	(D) supposed	(E) combined

_____ 1. To make a pudding, Peggy _____ sugar, milk, and eggs in a large bowl.

_____ 2. With the _____ of computers, people can deal with a large amount of data.

_____ 3. We _____ the tall woman was our new English teacher.

_____ 4. The author _____ to readers' opinions patiently.

_____ 5. It is dangerous to stand up from your seat when the bus is in _____.

III. 選擇題 (20%)

_____ 1. John lived a(n) _____ life in a small town, working at the local store.

    (A) elder   (B) ordinary   (C) blank   (D) younger

_____ 2. I always feel more confident and lighter after getting a fresh _____.

    (A) motion   (B) haircut   (C) gesture   (D) aid

_____ 3. In the opening _____, the prince had an argument with his father.

    (A) scene   (B) restroom   (C) roof   (D) zebra

_____ 4. The company values its _____, and provides a positive work environment for them.

    (A) umbrellas   (B) toilets   (C) socks   (D) employees

_____ 5. Jane handled her new phone in a careful _____ to avoid any damage.

    (A) worker   (B) cowboy   (C) manner   (D) gym

Level 2 Test 23

Class: _____ No.: _____ Name: _____ Score: _____

I. 文意字彙 (40%)

_____ 1. In the poem, Shakespeare c_____ed the woman he loved to a rose.

_____ 2. The girl handed out free s_____es of soap to everyone on the street.

_____ 3. Even though the old man owned great r_____s, he still led a simple life.

_____ 4. If you push this button, you'll see water flowing from the t_____e.

_____ 5. My son watches c_____ns on TV after school every day.

II. 字彙配合 (請忽略大小寫) (40%)

(A) peaceful	(B) hall	(C) selfish	(D) equal	(E) mask

_____ 1. The two students are _____ in their abilities to express themselves in English.

_____ 2. The theater _____ was crowded with people who wanted to see the famous actor.

_____ 3. I don't like Natalie because she is very _____ and never thinks of others.

_____ 4. If you've got the flu, you should wear a(n) _____ when you go to public places.

_____ 5. People living in war are dreaming of a(n) _____ life.

III. 選擇題 (20%)

_____ 1. The little girl drew a house with _____.

(A) crayons　　(B) engines　　(C) chips　　(D) masks

_____ 2. The _____ cost of the project turned out to be higher than expected.

(A) peaceful　　(B) actual　　(C) equal　　(D) selfish

_____ 3. For lunch, I ordered a delicious _____ with fries.

(A) panda　　(B) runner　　(C) hamburger　　(D) hall

_____ 4. Every morning, Matt _____ the floor to keep his house clean.

(A) aims　　(B) branches　　(C) bakes　　(D) sweeps

_____ 5. Local farmers grow potatoes in this _____.

(A) valley　　(B) employment　　(C) soda　　(D) motorcycle

Level 2 Test 24

Class: _____ No.: _____ Name: _____ Score: _____

I. 文意字彙 (40%)

_____ 1. If you want to tell me what has happened, please be b____f because I am in a hurry.

_____ 2. Most Chinese people think that c____ws are birds that will bring bad luck.

_____ 3. The young man felt confident in his h____e suit during the job interview.

_____ 4. The e____r decided to lay off ten workers in order to save money.

_____ 5. The singer c____ed the show with her favorite song.

II. 字彙配合 (請忽略大小寫) (40%)

(A) balcony	(B) mat	(C) stamp	(D) essay	(E) heaven

_____ 1. Have you read the _____ on the aging population in Taiwan?

_____ 2. The old lady believed that she would meet her dead husband in _____.

_____ 3. We can see the sea and beach from the _____ of our hotel room.

_____ 4. Don't forget to put a(n) _____ on the envelope before you send it.

_____ 5. The thief found the key hidden under the _____ and broke into the house.

III. 選擇題 (20%)

_____ 1. When the weather gets hot, many people choose to _____ at the beach.
(A) fry (B) swim (C) stamp (D) score

_____ 2. Jack invited me to be his dance _____ at the party.
(A) sandwich (B) defeat (C) turtle (D) partner

_____ 3. The lawyer charged a high _____ for his services.
(A) fee (B) peach (C) notebook (D) cock

_____ 4. Mary wrote her letter to Helen on a _____ of paper and placed it in an envelope.
(A) paradise (B) victory (C) rooster (D) sheet

_____ 5. Watching the cooking show on TV increased my _____, and I decided to cook for myself.
(A) castle (B) essay (C) appetite (D) adult

Level 2 Test 25

Class: _____ No.: _____ Name: _____ Score: _____

I. 文意字彙 (40%)

_____ 1. The teacher hit the c_____g when finding a student cheating on the exam.

_____ 2. Georgia burned the m_____t oil in order to hand in her history report on time.

_____ 3. Over time, the river can w_____h away the soil along its banks.

_____ 4. Rodney turned a d_____f ear to our advice and still went his own way.

_____ 5. The busy woman b_____ned the candle at both ends and finally got sick.

II. 字彙配合 (請忽略大小寫) (40%)

(A) highway	(B) emptied	(C) courage	(D) swing	(E) obeyed

_____ 1. After having failed for three times, Josh lost all his _____.

_____ 2. The father was watching his son playing on the _____ in the playground.

_____ 3. The driver got a ticket as a result of driving dangerously on the _____.

_____ 4. Julia _____ her backpack in order to look for her car key.

_____ 5. The soldier _____ the general's order without asking any questions.

III. 選擇題 (20%)

_____ 1. The friendly _____ helped us find our way back to the hotel.

    (A) stranger   (B) pear   (C) highway   (D) courage

_____ 2. It's considered _____ to talk loudly in a library.

    (A) scared   (B) rude   (C) beautiful   (D) empty

_____ 3. Jane _____ her favorite pictures into a large notebook.

    (A) obeyed   (B) hunted   (C) searched   (D) pasted

_____ 4. The project is divided into several _____, each with its own tasks.

    (A) balloons   (B) swings   (C) sections   (D) gardeners

_____ 5. Wendy is preparing to _____ for a job in the marketing department.

    (A) hike   (B) shine   (C) apply   (D) polish

Level 2

Level 2 Test 26

Class: _____ No.: _____ Name: _____ Score: _____

I. 文意字彙 (40%)

_____ 1. The heart is an important o_____n that controls the flow of blood around the body.

_____ 2. The p_____ws in the hotel room were so hard that Fanny didn't sleep well last night.

_____ 3. The small store only has a limited s_____n of furniture.

_____ 4. I can't a_____e this painting; I don't think it is beautiful.

_____ 5. The attack was said to be planned by a group of t_____ts.

II. 字彙配合 (請忽略大小寫) (40%)

(A) entrance	(B) path	(C) cream	(D) cage	(E) debt

_____ 1. The passing of the hikers has made a(n) _____ through the woods.

_____ 2. I am in _____ now, so I cannot return your money.

_____ 3. Wait for me at the _____ to the movie theater at 11 a.m.

_____ 4. Grace let the bird out of the _____ so that it could fly in the room.

_____ 5. Would you like some _____ in your coffee, sir?

III. 選擇題 (20%)

_____ 1. After a long day of work, I felt _____ and decided to go to bed earlier.

    (A) ill   (B) sleepy   (C) exact   (D) downstairs

_____ 2. Every evening, Jane _____ the kitchen floor to keep it clean.

    (A) mops   (B) cages   (C) realizes   (D) barbecues

_____ 3. This ruler is thirty _____ long.

    (A) hips   (B) geese   (C) paths   (D) centimeters

_____ 4. The phone's _____ was damaged when it fell on a hard surface.

    (A) screen   (B) strawberry   (C) sailor   (D) hippopotamus

_____ 5. Saving a little money every month can help you build _____ over time.

    (A) entrance   (B) credit   (C) wealth   (D) cream

Level 2 Test 27

Class: _____ No.: _____ Name: _____ Score: _____

I. 文意字彙 (40%)

_____ 1. Allen asked his b____r to give me a different hair cut.

_____ 2. Kent c____led his trip to New York City because he was ill.

_____ 3. Taking the medicine will help c____e you of your bad headache.

_____ 4. We've already known the truth. You can no longer d____y it.

_____ 5. The arguments have been s____ed in a friendly way; everything
will be fine.

II. 字彙配合 (請忽略大小寫) (40%)

| (A) independence | (B) secondary | (C) textbook | (D) grand | (E) pale |

_____ 1. Many people come to Nantou to enjoy the _____ view of Sun Moon Lake.

_____ 2. Diana forgot bringing her English _____, which made her teacher angry.

_____ 3. The girl's face turned _____ when she saw a spider in the toilet.

_____ 4. Students usually finish _____ school around the age of 18 in Taiwan.

_____ 5. The United States celebrates its _____ from Great Britain on July 4th.

III. 選擇題 (20%)

_____ 1. We need to _____ the box to make sure it is not too heavy.

    (A) hurry   (B) slide   (C) weigh   (D) vote

_____ 2. The car came to a _____ stop at the traffic light.

    (A) sudden   (B) humble   (C) secondary   (D) pale

_____ 3. David drew a picture on the wall with a piece of _____.

    (A) independence   (B) chalk   (C) excitement   (D) textbook

_____ 4. The _____ showed us the most expensive watch in the store.

    (A) ballot   (B) pizza   (C) mug   (D) salesperson

_____ 5. My kids dug a deep _____ in the sand at the beach.

    (A) eyebrow   (B) bakery   (C) hole   (D) artist

Level 2

Level 2 Test 28

Class: _____ No.: _____ Name: _____ Score: _____

I. 文意字彙 (40%)

_____ 1. Kate made an e____e about why she couldn't go to school today.

_____ 2. Can you p____n me for forgetting to give you a birthday gift?

_____ 3. The doctors are d_____ting if this drug is really good for patients.

_____ 4. Some parents i____t on giving their children the best education.

_____ 5. Anita was badly s____ked when seeing a serious car accident.

II. 字彙配合 (請忽略大小寫) (40%)

(A) platform	(B) poetry	(C) shame	(D) supper	(E) hero

_____ 1. Jeremy was so tired that he went to bed without having _____.

_____ 2. A lot of people are waiting impatiently on the _____, for the train has been half an hour late.

_____ 3. Patrick is regarded as a _____ for saving a girl's life from the big fire.

_____ 4. It's a _____ that my best friend Matilda can't come to my wedding.

_____ 5. This book tells us how to enjoy the beauty of _____.

III. 選擇題 (20%)

_____ 1. Jenny's dad bought her a _____ as her birthday gift.

(A) hero   (B) scooter   (C) fireman   (D) platform

_____ 2. My pen is out of _____. Can I borrow yours?

(A) depth   (B) ink   (C) supper   (D) shame

_____ 3. The musician played so well that we all _____ for her.

(A) defeated   (B) chased   (C) forgave   (D) cheered

_____ 4. Let's meet at the _____ for a drink after work.

(A) bar   (B) beat   (C) snail   (D) wheel

_____ 5. Craig works hard to earn a good _____ for his family.

(A) dinner   (B) waiter   (C) boo   (D) income

Level 2 Test 29

Class: _____ No.: _____ Name: _____ Score: _____

I. 文意字彙 (40%)

_____ 1. During the break, all the children went out of the classroom and played in the p____d.

_____ 2. Wilson and his friends used to b____e in this river during their childhood.

_____ 3. The country is struggling with some i____l affairs at the moment.

_____ 4. The b____ts go well with the coffee. I'd like to have one more piece.

_____ 5. Because of water and sunlight, life can e____t on earth.

II. 字彙配合 (請忽略大小寫) (40%)

(A) detail	(B) cheat	(C) dentist	(D) Internet	(E) poet

_____ 1. Judy went to the _____ this morning because she had a toothache.

_____ 2. The _____ is famous for his clever use of different languages.

_____ 3. You'll be a(n) _____ if you try to avoid paying taxes.

_____ 4. Ariel told me every single _____ of what she saw in Italy.

_____ 5. Ray surfed the _____ to read the latest news about his favorite sports team.

III. 選擇題 (20%)

_____ 1. The _____ caught a very big fish and became famous in his village.
(A) fisherman (B) cheat (C) tofu (D) detail

_____ 2. Ella didn't _____ her friend for the mistake; instead, she helped him fix it.
(A) silence (B) blame (C) jam (D) hop

_____ 3. Jane wore a simple _____ that went well with her dress.
(A) cookie (B) dentist (C) poet (D) necklace

_____ 4. A friendly _____ helped the lost child find her way home.
(A) seafood (B) quiet (C) policeman (D) Internet

_____ 5. John always keeps his _____ in the back pocket of his jeans.
(A) soybean (B) classmate (C) wolf (D) wallet

Level 2 Test 30

Class: _____ No.: _____ Name: _____ Score: _____

I. 文意字彙 (40%)

_____ 1. People waved f_____gs to greet their national heroes at the airport.

_____ 2. Victor s_____wed his coffee in a hurry and left the office.

_____ 3. Since we are not very rich, we have to avoid unnecessary e_____es when we are traveling.

_____ 4. I would rather watch TV than play c_____s tonight.

_____ 5. The handsome man who grows a b_____d is Lisa's husband.

II. 字彙配合 (請忽略大小寫) (40%)

(A) pork	(B) calendar	(C) needle	(D) meter	(E) trial

_____ 1. Christmas falls on the twenty-fifth day of the twelfth month on the _____.

_____ 2. The soldier was put on _____ for refusing to obey the general's orders.

_____ 3. If you want to park your car here, don't forget to feed the parking _____ with enough coins.

_____ 4. Siti is a Muslim, and she doesn't eat _____.

_____ 5. The nurse used a _____ to give the patient a flu shot.

III. 選擇題 (20%)

_____ 1. Sarah _____ the mouse and played her favorite song on the computer.

(A) poisoned   (B) jogged   (C) dialed   (D) clicked

_____ 2. This book is about an old _____ who lives in the mountains alone.

(A) hunter   (B) board   (C) needle   (D) calendar

_____ 3. Making a _____ about someone without knowing him or her well is not fair.

(A) spoon   (B) judgment   (C) meter   (D) workbook

_____ 4. The picnic basket was filled with cold _____, perfect for a hot day.

(A) trial   (B) division   (C) watermelon   (D) pork

_____ 5. I sent my friend a _____ from my vacation in Singapore.

(A) sidewalk   (B) seesaw   (C) postcard   (D) pavement

Level 2 Test 31

Class: _____ No.: _____ Name: _____ Score: _____

I. 文意字彙 (40%)

_____ 1. After retirement, my grandma moved from the city to the c____e to enjoy the beauty of nature.

_____ 2. It is the custom for Christians to p____y before having a meal.

_____ 3. At first, Andy denied taking the money, but he later a____tted it.

_____ 4. The accident happened because the worker i____ed the safety measures.

_____ 5. Lesley works very hard, for she believes her f____e is in her hands.

II. 字彙配合 (請忽略大小寫) (40%)

(A) domestic	(B) soft	(C) select	(D) joint	(E) childish

_____ 1. To save time, Zack did not plan to take the high-speed rail but booked a _____ flight.

_____ 2. It was very _____ of William to get angry about something so little.

_____ 3. The two companies are sure to survive the recession if they make a _____ effort.

_____ 4. Fur and feathers are _____ to touch. They are not hard at all.

_____ 5. Only a _____ few can become a member of the private club.

III. 選擇題 (20%)

_____ 1. Ian had a _____ after eating too much ice-cream.

    (A) bone   (B) lady   (C) stomachache   (D) prince

_____ 2. Sarah enjoyed a cold bottle of _____ on a summer day.

    (A) princess   (B) floor   (C) dialogue   (D) beer

_____ 3. The books cost 30 _____ each.

    (A) pounds   (B) miles   (C) weekdays   (D) sweaters

_____ 4. My grandma is 75 years old. She has long _____ hair.

    (A) mature   (B) silver   (C) joint   (D) domestic

_____ 5. Don't worry. I'll _____ the photos to the cloud tonight.

    (A) confess   (B) pour   (C) upload   (D) deny

Level 2

Level 2 Test 32

Class: _____ No.: _____ Name: _____ Score: _____

I. 文意字彙 (40%)

_____ 1. If you plant a seed in the s____l, it will grow day by day.

_____ 2. Molly showed me her w____g ring and told me she would get married next month.

_____ 3. This road is 100 meters b____d.

_____ 4. Only a m____y of people supported the new educational policy.

_____ 5. The s____t has been working for his master for more than 30 years.

II. 字彙配合 (請忽略大小寫) (40%)

(A) fault	(B) prayer	(C) nephew	(D) priest	(E) diary

_____ 1. Joan bought a model airplane for her _____ because he always dreamed of becoming a pilot.

_____ 2. The _____ is giving a speech at the Sunday church service.

_____ 3. Nancy kept a _____ during her childhood, in which she wrote down the things that happened to her every day.

_____ 4. Edward knelt down and said a _____ in the church.

_____ 5. The husband finds _____ with his wife all the time.

III. 選擇題 (20%)

_____ 1. The traffic is heavier than expected. I _____ if we'll make it on time.
(A) doubt　(B) beg　(C) print　(D) beg

_____ 2. Pauline bought a new _____ for the beach trip. She can't wait to try it on.
(A) keeper　(B) lap　(C) swimsuit　(D) whale

_____ 3. Becoming a successful cook requires a lot of cooking _____.
(A) nephews　(B) skills　(C) streams　(D) priests

_____ 4. Maria works hard to finish the project on time. Her sole _____ is meeting the deadline.
(A) concern　(B) majority　(C) journal　(D) curtain

_____ 5. The _____ view of the sunrise will stay in my memory forever.
(A) foolish　(B) narrow　(C) silly　(D) impressive

Level 2 Test 33

Class: _____ No.: _____ Name: _____ Score: _____

I. 文意字彙 (40%)

_____ 1. If you d____e with your manager, what should you do to make him accept your opinion?

_____ 2. P____s your finger against the button and the phone will be unlocked.

_____ 3. The audience c____ped for minutes when the show ended.

_____ 4. The p____r spent a year digging a tunnel underground and planning for his escape.

_____ 5. You may find a solution if you try to look at the problem from different a____es.

II. 字彙配合 (請忽略大小寫) (40%)

| (A) tales | (B) nerves | (C) consideration | (D) dragons | (E) principle |

_____ 1. Chinese kings used to wear robes with the images of _____.

_____ 2. The boss agreed to the plan in _____, but he didn't like some details.

_____ 3. You should take everything into _____ before you make a decision.

_____ 4. The car accident did great damage to Steve's spinal _____, and he wasn't able to walk ever since.

_____ 5. "Snow White" and "Cinderella" are both typical fairy _____.

III. 選擇題 (20%)

_____ 1. Before leaving the house, Katie quickly checked herself in the _____.
   (A) dancer　　(B) mirror　　(C) shark　　(D) brush

_____ 2. The study _____ that over 70% of the jobs in the village rely on fishing-related activities.
   (A) indicates　　(B) lays　　(C) slides　　(D) forgives

_____ 3. In the library, Tyler approached quietly to _____ in his sister's ear.
   (A) reflect　　(B) iron　　(C) whisper　　(D) stretch

_____ 4. As a _____, I started learning the basics of playing the piano.
   (A) fellow　　(B) beginner　　(C) nerve　　(D) rise

_____ 5. Sam squeezed the _____ bottle to add some flavor to his fries.
   (A) rumor　　(B) ketchup　　(C) brush　　(D) principle

Level 2

Level 2 Test 34

Class: _____ No.: _____ Name: _____ Score: _____

I. 文意字彙 (40%)

_____ 1. The monkey is so c____r that it will peel the banana before eating it.

_____ 2. The c____t will be valid as soon as you put your signature on it.

_____ 3. With great efforts, Amanda finally s____ded in becoming a famous actress.

_____ 4. Ian's office is d____t from his house. It takes him two hours to commute between them every day.

_____ 5. This notebook computer weights about one k____m.

II. 字彙配合 (請忽略大小寫) (40%)

| (A) lift | (B) painful | (C) journal | (D) protective | (E) printer |

_____ 1. Natalie's friend gave her a _____ to the office this morning.

_____ 2. The firefighter wore a _____ suit to shield against the heat.

_____ 3. A new laser _____ has been installed on the windows computer; it works much faster than the old one.

_____ 4. The athlete experienced a _____ injury during the game.

_____ 5. The scientist shared her discoveries in the scientific _____.

III. 選擇題 (20%)

_____ 1. The truck drivers couldn't see much in the thick _____.
(A) teapot (B) elevator (C) fog (D) niece

_____ 2. Benson measured the _____ of the bookshelf before buying it.
(A) drawing (B) pupil (C) shell (D) width

_____ 3. The flight experienced a _____, making passengers wait in the airport.
(A) delay (B) boil (C) ride (D) printer

_____ 4. Mrs. Wang likes to flavor her dishes with _____ and ginger.
(A) struggle (B) garlic (C) mist (D) drawing

_____ 5. I often drink red _____ when the main dish is pork or beef.
(A) shell (B) delay (C) width (D) wine

Level 2 Test 35

Class: _____ No.: _____ Name: _____ Score: _____

I. 文意字彙 (40%)

_____ 1. Seniors can do g_____e exercise to improve their strength and balance.

_____ 2. Parry wrote a love p_____m to admire the eyes of his lover.

_____ 3. Children usually don't like books with too much t_____t.

_____ 4. People in many countries are still suffering inequality. To them, social j_____e is a dream.

_____ 5. Ruby asked her brother to go d_____s to bring her a Coke.

II. 字彙配合 (請忽略大小寫) (40%)

(A) puzzled	(B) loaded	(C) earned	(D) divided	(E) tore

_____ 1. The farmer _____ the truck with freshly picked vegetables.

_____ 2. The county seems to be _____ into two groups. One likes the government, while the other doesn't.

_____ 3. The manager _____ the documents to pieces in a rage.

_____ 4. The old woman _____ a living by selling fruit in the market.

_____ 5. Karen was _____ by her cat's recent strange behavior.

III. 選擇題 (20%)

_____ 1. Larry went to the _____ to buy a new novel.

    (A) ladybug   (B) cell   (C) cloth   (D) bookstore

_____ 2. The _____ greeted us with a warm smile as we entered the store.

    (A) shopkeeper   (B) soul   (C) puzzle   (D) pudding

_____ 3. Tim was _____ for not completing the homework.

    (A) unloaded   (B) divided   (C) punished   (D) nodded

_____ 4. We decided to fly kites in a(n) _____ afternoon.

    (A) absent   (B) rough   (C) windy   (D) upstairs

_____ 5. The children were excited to find a _____ crawling on the flower in the backyard.

    (A) crime   (B) ladybug   (C) suit   (D) soul

Level 2

Level 2 Test 36

Class: _____ No.: _____ Name: _____ Score: _____

I. 文意字彙 (40%)

_____ 1. Jerry was promoted to director owing to his hard work and l_____p qualities.

_____ 2. Most of the g_____e in the dump can be recycled.

_____ 3. On closer e_____n, a bomb was found planted on the ceiling of the president's office.

_____ 4. The milk has gone s_____r. You should throw it away.

_____ 5. The c_____y sky indicates that it is going to rain.

II. 字彙配合 (請忽略大小寫) (40%)

(A) tissues	(B) customs	(C) rats	(D) wings	(E) drawers

_____ 1. Social _____ may be different from culture to culture.

_____ 2. The eagle spread its _____ and flew toward the sky.

_____ 3. Vera is cleaning out her _____, which are filled with old photos and magazines.

_____ 4. Can I have some _____? I need to blow my nose.

_____ 5. In the past, people kept cats to kill _____ in their houses or barns.

III. 選擇題 (20%)

_____ 1. It was reported that the actor had a(n) _____ with his fans.

    (A) shore   (B) pumpkin   (C) affair   (D) bun

_____ 2. The school has a strict no-cellphone _____ during class hours.

    (A) goat   (B) policy   (C) noodle   (D) lamb

_____ 3. The government is taking measures to prevent acts of _____ within the country.

    (A) rubbish   (B) custom   (C) quantity   (D) terrorism

_____ 4. Shanice wore a _____ layer of socks to keep her feet warm in the winter.

    (A) sweet   (B) solitary   (C) double   (D) lone

_____ 5. The _____ stole a wallet from the crowded market and quickly disappeared into the crowd.

    (A) ape   (B) thief   (C) cereal   (D) tissue

Level 2 Test 37

Class: _____ No.: _____ Name: _____ Score: _____

I. 文意字彙 (40%)

_____ 1. The stadium was thoroughly e_____ed before the president made a speech in it.

_____ 2. Please don't forget to put the milk in the r_____r, or it will turn sour.

_____ 3. I am very t____y. Can you give me a glass of water?

_____ 4. The train was delayed, and lots of passengers were waiting impatiently in the r_____d station.

_____ 5. Molly often a_____es with her husband about small things.

II. 字彙配合 (請忽略大小寫) (40%)

| (A) tongue | (B) album | (C) gentleman | (D) burden | (E) chapter |

_____ 1. The single father has to bear the _____ of raising his children on his own.

_____ 2. The _____ held the door open for the elderly woman entering the store.

_____ 3. Isabella collected the pictures of her Bali trip in this photograph _____.

_____ 4. Steve finished reading the first _____ of the novel before bedtime.

_____ 5. Spanish is Hugo's mother _____.

III. 選擇題 (20%)

_____ 1. We have to call a technician to check the machine because it _____ off by itself now and then.

(A) shuts   (B) tracks   (C) lends   (D) criticizes

_____ 2. Fred keeps _____ of current events around the world by reading online newspapers.

(A) cocoa   (B) purple   (C) track   (D) praise

_____ 3. _____ are Judy's favorite fruit.

(A) Dryers   (B) Doves   (C) Nuts   (D) Mangoes

_____ 4. Victor answered the question confidently on the _____ during the interview.

(A) lane   (B) spot   (C) wool   (D) railway

_____ 5. Whether the Wilson family will go camping or not _____ on the weather tomorrow.

(A) depend   (B) burden   (C) praise   (D) close

Level 2

Level 2 Test 38

Class: _____ No.: _____ Name: _____ Score: _____

I. 文意字彙 (40%)

_____ 1. On hearing the bad news, Mrs. Anderson b_____t out crying.

_____ 2. I think the beauty of the Grand Canyon is beyond d_____n.

_____ 3. People say that there is a large amount of buried t_____e in the cave.

_____ 4. Mr. Baker carried a l_____n through the woods, so he could see in the dark.

_____ 5. It is s_____y of William to believe what the salesman said.

II. 字彙配合 (請忽略大小寫) (40%)

(A) chart	(B) relation	(C) rubbed	(D) upset	(E) principal

_____ 1. Tammy's _____ reason for visiting the city is to look for investment opportunities.

_____ 2. From the temperature _____, the doctor can tell that the woman is pregnant.

_____ 3. Catherine _____ her hands, trying to make them warmer.

_____ 4. The manager's sudden illness _____ all the arrangements.

_____ 5. There is a close _____ between the moon and tides.

III. 選擇題 (20%)

_____ 1. The storm began to _____ loudly as dark clouds gathered in the sky.
   (A) exit   (B) rule   (C) thunder   (D) worm

_____ 2. The bag of sugar weighs 350 _____.
   (A) quizzes   (B) dramas   (C) grams   (D) operators

_____ 3. The hunter carefully aimed his _____ at the target.
   (A) ankle   (B) arrow   (C) liver   (D) cola

_____ 4. Cathy and Owen plan to _____ next summer in a beautiful garden ceremony.
   (A) rub   (B) dull   (C) govern   (D) marry

_____ 5. At the barbecue, Dad cooked the _____ to perfection and served it with potatoes.
   (A) chart   (B) steak   (C) diagram   (D) rub

Level 2 Test 39

Class: _____ No.: _____ Name: _____ Score: _____

I. 文意字彙 (40%)

_____ 1. Fill in the form if you want to apply for the m_____p of the gym.

_____ 2. The airline apologized for the late a_____l of the flight.

_____ 3. As soon as Vicky got home, she took off her high heels and put on her s_____rs.

_____ 4. Ken carried a b_____k on his trip, in which there was water, snacks, and a light jacket.

_____ 5. Shakespeare's plays are among the c_____cs of English literature.

II. 字彙配合 (請忽略大小寫) (40%)

(A) repair	(B) sail	(C) duty	(D) combed	(E) luck

_____ 1. I can't go to your birthday party because I will be on _____ tonight.

_____ 2. Although Kai didn't think he would win, he still tried his _____ anyway.

_____ 3. Matthew _____ out his hair before going out on a date.

_____ 4. The elevator is under _____, so we have to climb to our office on the tenth floor.

_____ 5. The Titanic set _____ on its maiden voyage on April 10th, 1912.

III. 選擇題 (20%)

_____ 1. Tony had a high _____, so he took some medicine and rested at home.

    (A) fever   (B) obligation   (C) eagle   (D) grape

_____ 2. The cat was _____ and wandered the street searching for food.

    (A) sailed   (B) promised   (C) mended   (D) deserted

_____ 3. The cheese was cut into some _____.

    (A) pajamas   (B) storms   (C) triangles   (D) tires

_____ 4. David put on his _____ when it started to rain.

    (A) duty   (B) lens   (C) grain   (D) raincoat

_____ 5. The man died from a gunshot _____ to his back.

    (A) departure   (B) wound   (C) repair   (D) promise

Level 2

Level 2 Test 40

Class: _____ No.: _____ Name: _____ Score: _____

I. 文意字彙 (40%)

_____ 1. A piece of c_____ l fell from the fire and burned the carpet.

_____ 2. You've won first prize in the speech contest. C_____ns on your achievement!

_____ 3. A strong e_____e destroyed the small town overnight.

_____ 4. To my surprise, Tina didn't r_____t my invitation.

_____ 5. Hana decided not to talk to Fred again because he had played a terrible t_____k on her.

II. 字彙配合 (請忽略大小寫) (40%)

(A) mood	(B) bend	(C) strike	(D) mention	(E) lid

_____ 1. Vincent can't even ride a bicycle, not to _____ a motorcycle.

_____ 2. Since Gill was not in the _____ for a movie, she chose to stay at home alone.

_____ 3. The runners _____ down to tie their shoelaces before heading out for a run.

_____ 4. The employees were on _____ in order to get higher salaries.

_____ 5. The movie star tried to avoid publicity and to keep a _____ on his private life.

III. 選擇題 (20%)

_____ 1. With efforts, Gary believes that his dream of becoming a doctor will come _____ one day.

(A) snowy (B) worst (C) true (D) false

_____ 2. The lady carefully chose a pair of _____ to go with her dress for the special occasion.

(A) pans (B) guavas (C) drugs (D) earrings

_____ 3. Alice spread jam on a piece of _____.

(A) toast (B) review (C) fox (D) trick

_____ 4. Helen and I had coffee and pasta at the _____.

(A) yam (B) strike (C) review (D) café

_____ 5. Diet, exercise, and sleep have often been _____ to one's overall health.

(A) toasted (B) accepted (C) related (D) drugged

基礎英文字彙力
2000
習題本

Answer Key

Level 1 Test 1
I. 1. fast 2. person 3. middle 4. place
   5. home
II. 1. C 2. B 3. E 4. D 5. A
III.1. C 2. B 3. D 4. A 5. D

Level 1 Test 2
I. 1. tripped 2. weather 3. class 4. first
   5. help
II. 1. E 2. C 3. A 4. D 5. B
III.1. A 2. D 3. C 4. C 5. B

Level 1 Test 3
I. 1. type 2. smell 3. both 4. nature
   5. appears
II. 1. B 2. E 3. D 4. C 5. A
III.1. B 2. A 3. D 4. C 5. A

Level 1 Test 4
I. 1. center 2. change 3. paper
   4. However 5. studies
II. 1. D 2. C 3. E 4. B 5. A
III.1. D 2. C 3. B 4. A 5. B

Level 1 Test 5
I. 1. airport 2. showed 3. explain
   4. ability 5. soon
II. 1. D 2. C 3. A 4. B 5. E
III.1. D 2. B 3. C 4. A 5. A

Level 1 Test 6
I. 1. exercise 2. away 3. already
   4. students 5. different
II. 1. B 2. D 3. E 4. A 5. C
III.1. A 2. B 3. D 4. C 5. B

Level 1 Test 7
I. 1. important 2. life 3. hope 4. next
   5. friendly
II. 1. A 2. C 3. E 4. D 5. B
III.1. B 2. D 3. A 4. B 5. C

Level 1 Test 8
I. 1. just 2. born 3. full 4. example
   5. main
II. 1. E 2. B 3. C 4. A 5. D
III.1. C 2. A 3. B 4. C 5. B

Level 1 Test 9
I. 1. music 2. live 3. Modern
   4. members 5. water
II. 1. C 2. D 3. E 4. A 5. B
III.1. C 2. B 3. A 4. D 5. D

Level 1 Test 10
I. 1. believed 2. time 3. even 4. public
   5. chocolate
iI. 1. E 2. C 3. A 4. B 5. D
III.1. A 2. B 3. D 4. C 5. B

Level 1 Test 11
I. 1. ever 2. fight 3. here 4. idea
   5. most
II. 1. B 2. E 3. A 4. C 5. D
III.1. B 2. D 3. C 4. D 5. A

Level 1 Test 12
I. 1. hand 2. year 3. last 4. half
   5. popular
II. 1. C 2. E 3. D 4. A 5. B
III.1. D 2. A 3. B 4. B 5. C

Level 1 Test 13
I. 1. second 2. enough 3. inside 4. rest
   5. almost
II. 1. B 2. E 3. C 4. A 5. D
III.1. A 2. B 3. D 4. C 5. B

Level 1 Test 14
I. 1. safe 2. rise 3. morning 4. national
   5. matter
II. 1. B 2. A 3. D 4. E 5. C
III.1. C 2. C 3. A 4. B 5. D

Level 1 Test 15
I. 1. once 2. ready 3. less 4. fresh
   5. season
II. 1. D 2. E 3. C 4. A 5. B
III.1. B 2. D 3. C 4. A 5. B

Level 1 Test 16
I. 1. plants 2. seeds 3. together
   4. report 5. famous
II. 1. C 2. D 3. A 4. E 5. B
III.1. A 2. C 3. B 4. A 5. D

Level 1 Test 17

I. 1. past 2. store 3. raised 4. service
5. certain

II. 1. D 2. B 3. C 4. E 5. A

III. 1. D 2. C 3. D 4. A 5. C

Level 1 Test 18

I. 1. outside 2. sentence 3. possible
4. restaurant 5. science

II. 1. B 2. A 3. E 4. D 5. C

III. 1. A 2. C 3. B 4. D 5. D

Level 1 Test 19

I. 1. understood 2. difficult 3. sure
4. Which 5. space

II. 1. D 2. B 3. A 4. C 5. E

III. 1. D 2. C 3. B 4. D 5. B

Level 1 Test 20

I. 1. allowed 2. early 3. traffic 4. visit
5. taste

II. 1. C 2. A 3. D 4. E 5. B

III. 1. A 2. B 3. B 4. A 5. B

Level 1 Test 21

I. 1. meeting 2. glasses 3. voice
4. hospital 5. homework

II. 1. C 2. A 3. E 4. D 5. B

III. 1. C 2. B 3. C 4. A 5. D

Level 1 Test 22

I. 1. somewhere 2. o'clock 3. visitors
4. grandfather 5. breakfast

II. 1. C 2. E 3. B 4. D 5. A

III. 1. A 2. D 3. C 4. A 5. B

Level 1 Test 23

I. 1. politely 2. guess 3. relatively
4. wake 5. interview

II. 1. E 2. B 3. C 4. A 5. D

III. 1. D 2. C 3. D 4. A 5. B

Level 1 Test 24

I. 1. medicine 2. sorry 3. afternoon
4. airplane 5. inviting

II. 1. C 2. A 3. E 4. D 5. B

III. 1. B 2. D 3. D 4. C 5. A

Level 1 Test 25

I. 1. rules 2. smoke 3. apartment
4. cousins 5. exciting

II. 1. E 2. C 3. A 4. B 5. D

III. 1. D 2. C 3. B 4. A 5. D

Level 1 Test 26

I. 1. Festival 2. baseball 3. popcorn
4. kitchen 5. driver

II. 1. C 2. B 3. A 4. E 5. D

III. 1. D 2. B 3. C 4. D 5. B

Level 1 Test 27

I. 1. arrived 2. basketball 3. wrong
4. decided 5. stupid

II. 1. D 2. C 3. A 4. E 5. B

III. 1. B 2. C 3. D 4. A 5. B

Level 1 Test 28

I. 1. pair 2. throat 3. factory 4. jacket
5. sleeping

II. 1. A 2. E 3. C 4. B 5. D

III. 1. D 2. C 3. B 4. D 5. A

Level 1 Test 29

I. 1. careful 2. pretty 3. farm 4. bottle
5. vegetables

II. 1. D 2. E 3. A 4. C 5. B

III. 1. D 2. A 3. C 4. B 5. D

Level 1 Test 30

I. 1. envelope 2. planet 3. terrible
4. pleasure 5. quick

II. 1. C 2. D 3. E 4. A 5. B

III. 1. D 2. D 3. C 4. C 5. B

Level 1 Test 31

I. 1. proud 2. correcting 3. kicked
4. ride 5. foreign

II. 1. D 2. A 3. E 4. C 5. B

III. 1. D 2. C 3. A 4. A 5. C

Level 1 Test 32

I. 1. window 2. foreigner 3. celebrated
4. repeat 5. cellphone

II. 1. E 2. D 3. A 4. B 5. C

III. 1. B 2. A 3. D 4. C 5. D

Level 1 Test 33

I. 1. Perhaps   2. husband   3. reporter
   4. temples   5. square
II. 1. C   2. E   3. A   4. B   5. D
III.1. C   2. B   3. A   4. C   5. A

Level 1 Test 34

I. 1. robots   2. ghost   3. monkeys
   4. letters   5. engineer
II. 1. B   2. D   3. C   4. E   5. A
III.1. C   2. D   3. B   4. C   5. A

Level 1 Test 35

I. 1. abroad   2. lose   3. coated   4. helpful
   5. towel
II. 1. A   2. E   3. C   4. B   5. D
III.1. D   2. A   3. B   4. C   5. D

Level 1 Test 36

I. 1. gray   2. misses   3. rainy
   4. treatment   5. convenient
II. 1. E   2. C   3. B   4. A   5. D
III.1. C   2. D   3. A   4. C   5. A

Level 1 Test 37

I. 1. except   2. listen   3. ring   4. surprise
   5. honest
II. 1. C   2. E   3. D   4. A   5. B
III.1. B   2. A   3. D   4. C   5. B

Level 1 Test 38

I. 1. count   2. teaching   3. expected
   4. Beans   5. surprised
II. 1. B   2. E   3. C   4. D   5. A
III.1. A   2. D   3. B   4. A   5. C

Level 1 Test 39

I. 1. loud   2. shower   3. tomatoes
   4. pencil   5. moment
II. 1. D   2. B   3. C   4. E   5. A
III.1. D   2. C   3. A   4. B   5. B

Level 1 Test 40

I. 1. Maybe   2. clock   3. tools
   4. telephone   5. defines
II. 1. C   2. E   3. B   4. D   5. A
III.1. C   2. B   3. D   4. D   5. A

Level 2 Test 1

I. 1. Thus   2. channels   3. following
   4. furniture   5. especially
II. 1. D   2. C   3. B   4. E   5. A
III.1. D   2. B   3. B   4. A   5. C

Level 2 Test 2

I. 1. beyond   2. delicious   3. therefore
   4. billion   5. society
II. 1. C   2. E   3. A   4. B   5. D
III.1. D   2. A   3. B   4. C   5. A

Level 2 Test 3

I. 1. university   2. generous   3. realize
   4. marriage   5. obvious
II. 1. B   2. D   3. E   4. A   5. C
III.1. B   2. A   3. C   4. D   5. C

Level 2 Test 4

I. 1. claimed   2. sensitive   3. religion
   4. active   5. nations
II. 1. C   2. D   3. A   4. E   5. B
III.1. D   2. A   3. D   4. B   5. C

Level 2 Test 5

I. 1. escape   2. address   3. emphasizes
   4. founded   5. guard
II. 1. C   2. E   3. A   4. B   5. D
II. 1. B   2. D   3. A   4. C   5. D

Level 2 Test 6

I. 1. encouraged   2. organization
   3. medical   4. complex   5. couple
II. 1. E   2. A   3. B   4. C   5. D
II. 1. B   2. D   3. A   4. C   5. D

Level 2 Test 7

I. 1. conversation   2. extra   3. avoid
   4. greets   5. ancient
II. 1. A   2. D   3. C   4. B   5. E
III.1. A   2. C   3. A   4. D   5. B

Level 2 Test 8

I. 1. education   2. describe   3. population
   4. peace   5. further
II. 1. B   2. C   3. E   4. D   5. A
III.1. C   2. B   3. A   4. D   5. C

Level 2 Test 9
I. 1. identity   2. solve   3. instruments
   4. prefers   5. cancer
II. 1. E   2. C   3. A   4. B   5. D
II. 1. D   2. A   3. C   4. B   5. D

Level 2 Test 10
I. 1. developed   2. chemicals   3. former
   4. expression   5. introduction
II. 1. D   2. A   3. C   4. B   5. E
III.1. B   2. A   3. C   4. D   5. A

Level 2 Test 11
I. 1. clothing   2. source   3. golden   4. loss
   5. activity
II. 1. C   2. E   3. A   4. B   5. D
III.1. D   2. B   3. B   4. A   5. C

Level 2 Test 12
I. 1. discovered   2. general   3. alone
   4. technology   5. measured
II. 1. A   2. E   3. D   4. C   5. B
III.1. C   2. B   3. D   4. A   5. B

Level 2 Test 13
I. 1. considered   2. central   3. better
   4. universe   5. solution
II. 1. D   2. C   3. B   4. E   5. A
III.1. D   2. A   3. C   4. B   5. D

Level 2 Test 14
I. 1. approaching   2. cultural   3. accept
   4. influence   5. opinion
II. 1. D   2. E   3. C   4. B   5. A
III.1. C   2. A   3. D   4. A   5. C

Level 2 Test 15
I. 1. legal   2. standard   3. international
   4. Environmental   5. highly
II. 1. D   2. A   3. E   4. B   5. C
III.1. A   2. D   3. B   4. C   5. D

Level 2 Test 16
I. 1. terms   2. position   3. aircraft
   4. increase   5. links
II. 1. E   2. B   3. C   4. A   5. D
III.1. B   2. A   3. C   4. C   5. D

Level 2 Test 17
I. 1. musical   2. survived   3. trade   4. lack
   5. mixture
II. 1. C   2. B   3. D   4. A   5. E
III.1. D   2. B   3. A   4. C   5. D

Level 2 Test 18
I. 1. objected   2. addition   3. produces
   4. attempted   5. fashion
II. 1. C   2. B   3. A   4. E   5. D
III.1. B   2. C   3. D   4. A   5. B

Level 2 Test 19
I. 1. wonder   2. rather   3. search   4. edge
   5. company
II. 1. B   2. C   3. A   4. D   5. E
III.1. A   2. D   3. B   4. C   5. C

Level 2 Test 20
I. 1. control   2. damage   3. result
   4. respect   5. available
II. 1. C   2. E   3. A   4. D   5. B
III.1. B   2. A   3. D   4. C   5. D

Level 2 Test 21
I. 1. absence   2. replied   3. satisfy
   4. worth   5. rent
II. 1. D   2. C   3. B   4. A   5. E
III.1. C   2. A   3. B   4. C   5. B

Level 2 Test 22
I. 1. badminton   2. trap   3. friendships
   4. password   5. electrical
II. 1. E   2. C   3. D   4. B   5. A
III.1. B   2. B   3. A   4. D   5. C

Level 2 Test 23
I. 1. compared   2. samples   3. riches
   4. tube   5. cartoons
II. 1. D   2. B   3. C   4. E   5. A
III.1. A   2. B   3. C   4. D   5. A

Level 2 Test 24
I. 1. brief   2. crows   3. handsome
   4. employer   5. concluded
II. 1. D   2. E   3. A   4. C   5. B
III.1. B   2. D   3. A   4. D   5. C

Level 2 Test 25
I. 1. ceiling   2. midnight   3. wash   4. deaf
   5. burned
II. 1. C   2. D   3. A   4. B   5. E
III. 1. A   2. B   3. D   4. C   5. C

Level 2 Test 26
I. 1. organ   2. pillows   3. selection
   4. appreciate   5. terrorists
II. 1. B   2. E   3. A   4. D   5. C
III. 1. B   2. A   3. D   4. A   5. C

Level 2 Test 27
I. 1. barber   2. cancel(l)ed   3. cure
   4. deny   5. settled
II. 1. D   2. C   3. E   4. B   5. A
III. 1. C   2. A   3. B   4. D   5. C

Level 2 Test 28
I. 1. excuse   2. pardon   3. debating
   4. insist   5. shocked
II. 1. D   2. A   3. E   4. C   5. B
III. 1. B   2. B   3. D   4. A   5. D

Level 2 Test 29
I. 1. playground   2. bathe   3. internal
   4. biscuits   5. exist
II. 1. C   2. E   3. B   4. A   5. D
III. 1. A   2. B   3. D   4. C   5. D

Level 2 Test 30
I. 1. flags   2. swallowed   3. expenses
   4. chess   5. beard
II. 1. B   2. E   3. D   4. A   5. C
III. 1. D   2. A   3. B   4. C   5. C

Level 2 Test 31
I. 1. countryside   2. pray   3. admitted
   4. ignored   5. fate
II. 1. A   2. E   3. D   4. B   5. C
III. 1. C   2. D   3. A   4. B   5. C

Level 2 Test 32
I. 1. soil   2. wedding   3. broad   4. minority
   5. servant
II. 1. C   2. D   3. E   4. B   5. A
III. 1. A   2. C   3. B   4. A   5. D

Level 2 Test 33
I. 1. disagree   2. Press   3. clapped
   4. prisoner   5. angles
II. 1. D   2. E   3. C   4. B   5. A
III. 1. B   2. A   3. C   4. B   5. B

Level 2 Test 34
I. 1. clever   2. contract   3. succeeded
   4. distant   5. kilogram
II. 1. A   2. D   3. E   4. B   5. C
III. 1. C   2. D   3. A   4. B   5. D

Level 2 Test 35
I. 1. gentle   2. poem   3. text   4. justice
   5. downstairs
II. 1. B   2. D   3. E   4. C   5. A
III. 1. D   2. A   3. C   4. C   5. B

Level 2 Test 36
I. 1. leadership   2. garbage
   3. examination   4. sour   5. cloudy
II. 1. B   2. D   3. E   4. A   5. C
III. 1. C   2. B   3. D   4. C   5. B

Level 2 Test 37
I. 1. examined   2. refrigerator   3. thirsty
   4. railroad   5. argues
II. 1. D   2. C   3. B   4. E   5. A
III. 1. A   2. C   3. D   4. B   5. A

Level 2 Test 38
I. 1. burst   2. description   3. treasure
   4. lantern   5. silly
II. 1. E   2. A   3. C   4. D   5. B
III. 1. C   2. C   3. B   4. D   5. B

Level 2 Test 39
I. 1. membership   2. arrival   3. slippers
   4. backpack   5. classics
II. 1. C   2. E   3. D   4. A   5. B
III. 1. A   2. D   3. C   4. D   5. B

Level 2 Test 40
I. 1. coal   2. Congratulations
   3. earthquake   4. reject   5. trick
II. 1. D   2. A   3. B   4. C   5. E
III. 1. C   2. D   3. A   4. D   5. C